A Love for Doctor
Mary Taylor

Ana C. Sales

5310 publishing

A Love for Doctor Mary Taylor

Romance by Ana C. Sales

Published by

5310 Publishing Company

5310publishing.com

Our books may be purchased in bulk for promotional, educational, or business use. Please contact your local bookseller or 5310 Publishing at sales@5310publishing.com.

ISBN Paperback: 978-1-990158-26-1

ISBN Ebook: 978-1-990158-27-8

Author: Ana C. Sales

Editor: Alex Williams

Cover design: Eric Williams

First edition (this edition) released in November 2021.

For you, dear reader, who loves to read just like me.

Reading a good book leads you to a new and unknown world, full of dreams and illusions.

-Ana C. Sales

A Ponte Que Eu Não Atravessei (2019)
The Greystones - Fall in love with them. (2021)

Chapter One

Paul arrived at his apartment and saw the answering machine flashing. You have three messages. He pressed the button.

First message: "Paul, it's me, your mother; I need to talk to you. Call me when you arrive. Kisses with love."

Second message: "Paul, I called several times on your cell phone, you don't answer. I miss you... — when can we see each other again? Kisses." Andrea.

Third message: "Paul, this is Wagner. I need to talk to you urgently, something came up, can you call me? Thank you." The first message could wait. After all, his mother always needed to talk.

The second one no longer interested him. Andrea was becoming tiresome.

He had to call the third one back. Wagner, besides being a great friend, was also his "compadre." Paul was the baptismal godfather of Wagner's eldest son, Mark.

He picked up the phone to dial but decided to take off

his suit first and take a shower. He was exhausted... It couldn't be anything so serious. He could wait.

He went to his all-male room with tasteful and quality furniture.

There was a king-size bed, covered with a dark green bedspread and three beautiful matching pillows.

The walls were lined with imported wallpaper, and there was a large mirror on the right side. He could see himself when he was lying down and also when he took someone to his apartment.

Usually, he enjoyed going to hotels, which are more impersonal, but nothing would stop him from having a company there, where he considered to be a sacred den.

He entered his huge closet, which was located behind his bed separated only by a wall made especially for that purpose, and when he began to untie the tie knot, his cell phone rang in his pocket.

Damn, he thought annoyed. I don't have peace even when I get home.

"Hello!" he said in a dry voice.

"Man, I've been trying to reach you for hours," Wagner said impatiently.

"You're not answering your DAMN phone."

"Hi, buddy, I was about to call you. I just saw your message; I've just walked into my apartment. The phone was dead, and I charged it in the car. Is everything alright?" He didn't mind the outburst, he'd known his friend for years, and he knew something was wrong.

He felt tension on the other side of the line and began to worry. He was about to speak again when Wagner said. "My son was arrested, help me..." and began to cry.

"Calm down, man, I'm coming. Where are you?"

"We're at the twelfth precinct. Can you come now?" asked his friend eagerly and in tears.

"Sure! I'm on my way. Hang on, I'll be there in 15 minutes, tops. Tell Mark not to say anything.

"Bye!!"

Paul ran down the stairs, took the jacket and car keys and rushed out to the elevator.

Traffic at that time was calm. And at most in fifteen minutes, he would be by his childhood friend's side as he had predicted. As he stopped at the red light, he started wondering what Mark had done this time.

He didn't like judging others, but it was the second time in four months. Was it going to become a routine? he thought upset.

The first time there was a robbery, and Mark was in the wrong place at the wrong time. What now? What could it be?

He stopped in the parking space in front of the twelfth police precinct, quickly got off the car and got in the building.

Nothing would prepare him for the shock he felt when he saw his friend's face. He was unsettled by the pain, the suffering totally exposed, his eyes scared and red.

He approached his friend, who looked at him with tears in his eyes. At the same time, Wagner threw himself into his arm, in a tight embrace.

"Where's Mark, Wagner?" he asked seriously.

"Inside with the police," he replied sniffing.

"I'm going there! Wait for me here. I'll be right back."

He walked up to a huge counter and identified himself as Mark's lawyer. At once, the officer on duty referred him to the interrogation room.

"Good evening." he entered uninvited.

The officer stood up and greeted him with a handshake.

He put his hand on Mark's shoulder and squeezed it. "Everything all right, buddy?" he said fondly.

He looked at Paul with red eyes. Paul looked at the cop. "Can you fill me in on the situation, please?" he was extremely polite.

The officer spoke politely, "Sir, wait just a moment. The chief is already coming. I was here talking off-the-record with the boy. Excuse me." The officer left the room.

Paul looked at his friend's son.

"Can you tell me what happened?" he said calmly.

Mark looked at him with the same light brown eyes of his friend.

"We were at Pier 21 at Attila restaurant and there was a fight beside our table, and a guy killed the another in front of us." His voice was choking and his eyes moist. "The police came and arrested me. I'm being accused, but I didn't do it, Uncle Paul, I swear to you." He started crying like a child, putting his hands on his face.

"How did they kill the guy?" he asked calmly. Mark was about to answer, but before he did, the chief came in.

"Good evening!" Already reaching out his hand to Paul.

Paul shook the chief's hand and could see in his eyes that he was a good person.

"The boy here was arrested because the cops recognized him from a previous fight, but it's just a misunderstanding and you're cleared. Everything has been clarified."

He looked directly at Paul and said:

"I advise you to instruct your client to stay out of trouble. He's already got priors, and wherever he is, he's always going to be the suspect. Unfortunately, our justice system is like that and there is nothing we can do about it. I appreciate the understanding, and I apologize for the inconvenience of making you come here, but as you know, in a murder case everything must be analyzed."

Paul looked at the chief with tired eyes and sympathized with him.

"All right, thank you, sir. Have a good night." He shook his hand.

"Good night! I don't know if it's going to be a quiet night. We've been having a lot of violence lately," the chief said in a calm voice.

"And you boy," the chief said looking at Mark. "Value your life, show your father some respect. He is truly devastated by all this. We often look for problems. Your life is good, and you should rethink it. Good luck!" he shook Mark's hand and opened the door for the two of them to leave.

As soon as they left, Wagner got up with a jump and

came to meet them.

He squeezed his son into his arms. "Everything all right? Are you alright?"

"Can we just go? What happened in there?" anxiety and despair were clear in the voice and expression of his best friend.

Paul held Wagner's arm and said:

"Let's get out of here. I'll explain outside." He spoke and was already leading them both out the door.

They left the police station and stopped next to Paul's car in the parking lot.

"It was just a misunderstanding," he spoke quietly. "Mark was at the Attila on Pier 21 and there was a murder inside, but everything has been cleared. You can go home." Paul spoke wearily.

Wagner looked at him seriously and said:

"Paul, is that right? To arrest a person without proof and to make us come here, go through all this stress and then release him, just with an apology? Should we sue them?"

Paul looked at his friend, tired and downcast, struggling to raise his three children all by himself after his wife's death, and felt somewhat proud of him.

"Wagner, Mark has been booked by the police, and more than once has been involved in fights and bar arguments. The chief was very friendly and released us without further problems. It's best not to stir up a hornet's nest. We are free and we can go home to rest."

He looked at his friend's son with his head down, who he

had known since he was born and felt bad for him. He touched his fallen shoulder and said softly.

"Go home with your father, Mark, and think about what the chief's told you just now. If you are given advice, if it is good, you should follow it. Your father has been doing his best for you, but I see that somehow, he has failed you, and I don't think you make things easier for him either. Rethink your life. You're almost eighteen. I think it's time you make this guy who loves you most of anything proud, and your mother would be proud if you could change. I'll always be here for you, but I'm not God. If you fuck up at 18, I won't be able to get you out easily, and you should know that our justice system is flawed and not moral at all. Be smart, man! Do not make your father suffer more than you have already had to. Life is too short."

Mark looked at his godfather and murmured ashamed.

"Thank you, Uncle Paul. I promise you, I'm going to do it differently this time, and my mom will be able to be proud of me."

Will you forgive me, Dad? I love you, and I know it's been hard for you without Mom and on top of that, you have me giving you a hard time, but I promise to behave from now on because I've learned my lesson. "I've never been so scared in my life."

Wagner hugged his son with love.

"We'll talk tomorrow, Wagner, take him home and get some rest too. You look awful." Paul said smiling with his eyes.

"Thanks, buddy. I'll stop by your office tomorrow to settle everything. You look horrible too," he said with a smile.

"Forget it, you know I'm not going to charge you, but come by anyway so we can talk."

He hugged his friend tightly and then he hugged his friend's son, messing up his hair that needed a good cut.

"Behave, huh?" He didn't know why, but this time Paul believed in Mark.

They all said goodbye and went home. Paul took a glimpse at the car's clock that showed 9:00 p.m. He needed a shower, a light meal, and a good night's sleep.

The day had been tiring, and he longed to relax in his apartment.

While driving home, Paul was reflecting on his day.

He was both worn out and very happy. They had won another battle against a ruthless and self-centered millionaire.

The hearing took longer than expected and he would still have to go through some aspects to further improve his client's situation. Fortunately, the judge had agreed to joint custody. It could be worse.

After two long years of bickering, many impositions and arguments, now everything could be calmer for Helen, his client, and her children.

Often, being a lawyer is stressful and the pressure is too much, but when you win a case, it's all worth it, Paul thought.

When he was hired to solve a problem, he always struggled to do his best, thus ensuring that the client was satisfied with his performance and he could be proud of who he was.

And hasn't it always been like that? he thought ironically.

Paul took his career very seriously and liked to know that he could make a difference with people and collaborate so that there was justice. But justice was not always served. Every judge thought in a different way and when he couldn't get good results, he got frustrated and blamed himself thinking he hadn't done his best.

He considered himself real lucky; he was tall, about six point four feet tall, one hundred and ninety-eight pounds very well distributed, dark brown hair and large blue eyes. His eyebrows were thick, and once a month, he had the excess hair removed so that they would look more beautiful. You could say he was a metrosexual. So what? He never knew that wanting to look nice and being vain was a sin. Beauty was not exclusive to women.

He loved to change his look, he grew a beard, shaved it, grew a mustache, goatee and whatever else he could, but always very clean, he made a point of that.

Looks were everything, especially in the profession where he needed to convey confidence and credibility, he thought smiling.

His suits were all made in the best tailoring in town, and the shoes he made a point of being handmade and Italian: comfort and quality.

Despite living well, being vain and going around super well dressed, once a month, he participated in the distribution of food for the poor in the city center.

A group of twelve people made some of their time available to help the less fortunate.

Homeless people, who lived on the margins of society, where many come and go and pretend not to see or hear them. Paul liked to know that at least once every month he could help them and always longed for those moments.

Through this small gesture, he expressed his love for others and reciprocated everything he received from God and his family.

Not everyone had the privilege of being born into a well-structured family and having such loving parents. He was lucky, so the way to make up for it was this, helping and serving others more and more.

It was through a friend, Amanda, also a lawyer, that Paul met the group "Helping the Less Fortunate," he was invited to take part for the first time in the soup kitchen, as it is called, when one of the members became ill and could not attend it, so eleven people, became twelve, with his total dedication.

He decided to collaborate with the group two years after losing his older brother, John, to a cocaine overdose.

He and his family went through moments of pure terror and frustration when they couldn't help his brother, so every person he could get off the streets, drugs or even prostitution and bring a word of comfort and solidarity to was worth it. He saw his brother in each one of them. He wasn't perfect, but he always tried to be serious and, above all, to be charitable.

As he drove home, he thought of his brother. It had been four years since he had passed away, and Paul and his family had not yet become used to it.

His brother was wonderful, witty, and funny. The kind of

person everyone wants around, he was agitated in his way of being and never denied people anything. Whatever it was, John would find a way to help. But unfortunately, the physical education teacher at the school, we never think of the teacher as someone who would encourage young people to abuse substances. No one could ever imagine that the teacher himself, someone you trust, would offer drugs to a student. But that is what happened, and the end was super sad and distressing, both for John and for everyone in the family.

It was especially for their father, a retired Federal Marshal. He always fought drugs and tried not to make it easy for drug dealers.

I hate drug dealers, he thought upset. As much as he tried to accept that everyone does what they want in life, he would not accept that there were no harsher penalties and that they really worked.

More and more the world was being plagued with drugs, and every day, different and more potent drugs appeared. At the time, the use of crack was prevailing, and addicts looked more like zombies, so they took the name "freaks" for not sleeping at night in search of five seconds of pleasure.

Paul diverted his thoughts to other things. These reflections only made him sad and depressed.

He once again was delighted when he entered his street.

It was all tree-lined with beautiful oak trees in different shades of green, and when they flourished, it was a real work of art.

The traffic was already very quiet at that time of night. He went straight to his apartment, a huge penthouse in one of the noblest areas of the city. He always knew that living well would be a matter of principle, and he wouldn't give that up.

Chapter Two

The hospital was full, and Mary went straight up to the operating room. Motorcycle accidents were the most common.

She was competent and fast.

"Good morning Dr. Taylor," said her assistant cheerfully.

"Good morning!" replied Mary.

The surgery wasn't long, and everything went well. In a few days, the patient would already be at home and with several scars on the abdomen.

The car that hit the biker got him in full. It was a real miracle that he was alive.

"How's our schedule today?" she asked while taking off her gloves.

"You have two more surgeries today."

"Do I have time for coffee?" she asked smiling.

"Sure! I'll have the patient brought in. You have half an hour."

"Okay, thank you, Patty."

Mary was sweet and very capable. Her efficiency in doing surgeries was being appreciated by everyone in the hospital.

She was quick and accurate with the scalpel.

She went down the elevator with two other people, but she didn't pay attention. She was checking her messages on her cell phone.

I need to call Mom, she thought.

She walked into the crowded diner and made a small sign for her server friend. He already knew what she wanted and made a positive sign with his finger. Mary thanked him with a smile and waited.

"Good morning, Dr. Taylor!" said Dr. Robson joyfully.

"Good morning!" she replied smiling.

"Can I keep you company, Mary?" he asked cheerfully pulling a chair.

"Sure! How are things? Busy, huh?" she said keeping her cell phone in her lab coat pocket.

"Tell me about it, honey. I think they all decided to get sick."

He spoke looking into her green eyes.

Robson was a great cardiologist, but he didn't do surgeries.

"That's true. I still have two more surgeries today, and I just got out of one."

"How can you be so beautiful?" asked Robson suddenly.

"I was born this way," Mary replied with a large smile, and he also smiled, loving those fleshy lips.

"How about we go out tomorrow? Dinner out or just relax having a glass of wine?" he asked hopefully.

The server brought her order. Mary paid with the card and was already eating fast.

"I'm so tired, Robson. Let's take a rain check, okay?"

she said rising from her chair and giving her friend an affectionate kiss on the cheek.

"Okay, baby. As you wish," he replied annoyed and with a pale smile.

Mary left in a hurry.

Robson leaned back in his chair and thought of Mary. They'd been out a few times and the sex was always good. But Mary didn't seem to want anything serious, he thought frustrated.

He had known Mary for two years and was in love with her. He had never declared himself, but attitudes say more than words, right? he thought.

He wanted someone like Mary: smart, independent, and caring. Would that be too much to ask? I don't think I'll ever have a chance with her, he said mentally.

Mary had had an exhaustingly hectic day.

She was a beautiful doctor, general surgeon, brunette, very black hair, green eyes, tall and slender. Since she worked twelve to fourteen hours a day, she barely had time to eat.

She was a practical and independent woman. The daughter of a single mother, she was raised without a father figure and with her feet on the ground, very much within the reality of what life was like. Her mother never overlooked her mistakes.

If she was independent today, it was because she had to struggle to get where she was.

She came home exhausted and hungry. It was after 8:50

p.m. She had been living in her new apartment for five months and felt super happy. She thought she was lucky to live so well in a high-end apartment.

There was hardly any noise from the neighbors and she rarely met anyone in the elevators or in the garage.

With the busy life she led when she got home, she just wanted a warm bath, something to eat, and a bed.

She didn't have a boyfriend, and she didn't mean to have one soon. That kind of relationship just got in the way.

She enjoyed her single life and not having to give satisfaction to anyone. She was her own woman and intended to stay that way for a long time.

She'd been struggling with the door lock for ten minutes and decided to go to the lobby to ask the doorman to accompany her and try to open that damn door.

She waited for the elevator, and when it arrived, she came face to face with a man elegantly dressed and with an unfriendly face.

"Good evening!" greeted Mary.

"Good evening," Paul answered politely after a few seconds.

"Do you live here?" he asked.

"Yes. I'm going to the lobby to ask for help, my lock has stuck, and the key does not go in. I am so tired... Oh! God! I'm so sorry, I did not want to unload my frustrations on you. Oh, we're going up!" The annoyance in her face and voice was clear.

Paul just smiled. "My name is Paul and I live in the

penthouse. That's why we're going up."

What a snob! she thought without saying a word.

"Do you want me to help you?" he asked more out of politeness because he was super tired and would not want to help anyone. He just wanted to go home as soon as possible.

"Thank you so much," replied Mary without even looking him in his face.

"I'll call whoever knows these things." She said and looked at him from top to bottom.

How rude! thought Paul annoyed.

"OK." was his short answer.

The elevator stopped on his floor and Paul got out, saying good night in a weak voice. Without waiting for an answer and already picking up his key, he barely looked into Mary's face.

Mary went down even more upset than she already was, as she had to climb up to the twenty-seventh floor and now she would have to go down all over again.

What a setback, she thought dismally. So pompous 'I live in the penthouse, so we're going up,' she imitated Paul.

The doorman was very polite and called another evening employee to sub for him while he accompanied Dr. Taylor.

Without much difficulty, the door was opened, and Mary politely thanked the doorman, insisting on tipping him.

"Thank you very much, Dr. Taylor." He said in a humble smile.

"Good night!" replied Mary smiling as well.

Tomorrow I will arrange to change this lock to avoid further annoyances, thought Mary closing the door and breathing relieved.

She took a long, relaxing shower, heated something that the cleaner had left in the fridge, and ate with gusto. She couldn't tell if it was chicken or fish, but it was great.

She poured a glass of wine and sat in a comfortable armchair on her spacious balcony.

The moon was wonderful, and she was able to relax there.

She remembered the man in the elevator. *Handsome!* she thought smiling. *Handsome and conceited*, she smiled again.

She kept thinking that if she weren't so tired and upset about that damn lock, she might have flirted with the handsome man from the penthouse. She smiled as she imagined it. *How long would I have?* she thought.

She collected the glass and went to her room to sleep. By the time she laid her head on the pillow, she had closed her eyes and instantly fell deeply asleep.

Mary woke up with the alarm clock and took a deep breath. She said her prayers thanking God for another day of life and asked for numerous blessings over the course of the new day.

The weeks flew by, and after two and a half months, Mary met Paul in the elevator again.

"Good evening!" he said politely.

"Good evening!" she answered by looking into his eyes.

"Are you a doctor?" asked Paul reading her name on the lab coat.

"Yes," she replied with a smile.

"Tired?" he asked.

"Exhausted," she replied.

"Good night! This is me."

"Good night! " answered Paul watching her beautiful ass.

The elevator closed and Paul imagined making love to her. He smiled shaking his head; *what an imagination!* He thought to himself smiling and finding his sinful thoughts amusing.

Paul arrived at his penthouse and everything was clean and smelling good; his cleaning lady really was diligent and deserved the salary she earned. Everything was impeccably clean and in order.

He took off his tie and washed his hands well. He took something from the fridge and heated it in the microwave, he ate it not knowing what it was, but it was very good.

Chapter Three

"Paul? Is that you?" He heard as he approached his colleague, Debby. "Is everything all right?"

"Hi Debby, everything is fine, how about you?" He looked at her in an amusing way.

"I'm as usual," she said with a smile, "a bit stressed had a hearing all day today, and I'm still taking work home."

"Lawyer's life," she said smiling. "Isn't that what we wanted so badly? We longed to have the phone ringing all the time, and now we want to throw it against the wall."

"Can I give you a word of advice, Debby?" he asked without waiting for an answer.

"Go home, take a nice shower, then pour a glass of wine and relax. Tomorrow is going to be a new day."

Debby looked at him with her beautiful honey-colored eyes and said, "you are always so...so...chill. How can you not get stressed? I wish I could be so calm, you know?"

Paul smiled charmingly, "take it easy, baby. You'll get there."

They gave a naughty smile and said goodbye with a

gentle kiss on the cheeks.

Debby was smart, fun, and very beautiful. Terrific lawyer!

He worked in the labor law field and could not bear employees who wanted at all costs to squeeze money from the employer. She used to say that, unfortunately, labor justice did not always do justice. He often agreed with her.

He packed his backpack for the next day. It was soup kitchen day and he always changed clothes before leaving the office and going with his friends in an old van with holes on the sides.

By 7:00 p.m. he was already getting ready to go out with his friends for the soup kitchen.

Paul changed his clothes and gave his car keys to the boy in charge of leaving the car in the garage of his house and his belongings in his penthouse. He had been working with Paul for five years and was extremely reliable.

"Let's go," he said excitedly to the people inside the old van.

Upon arriving, they noticed that the city center was more crowded than the previous month. Each day the number of homeless increased more and more and the government seemed to be unaware of the situation. It was extremely degrading to see so many young and old people walking aimlessly, hopelessly and taking no notice of what was going on around them.

"Hey, Paul, everything all right, man?" his friend Wagner was excited and happy to make a difference.

"All right, man. What about you?" he said with a smile as

he picked up tables to set up one by one. It was always the same, they put together several plastic tables to form a large line and put their large pots of soup, bread loaves, salted pies and some sweets; often leftovers from parties and events from the rich that they would give as donations to the soup kitchen. But there wasn't always candy.

They tried not to decorate too much and give false hope to the homeless. Once in a while, there were those wonderful sweets.

"Wagner, can you pass the towels, please? " asked Paul politely.

"Man, the situation here is getting worse every day!" as he passed the towels, he talked and looked around. Paul looked into Wagner's eyes and was also sad.

"Yes, and the government doesn't do anything."

"Often too, these people don't want to go to shelters or go back to their depressing and violent homes. They prefer to live on the street." Wagner said.

"Remember that census they did once? They didn't want to go back home." Paul spoke as he quickly put away things.

A line was already forming and the homeless began to get impatient.

The twelve friends passed the dishes, and each filled the dish with some food. Paul was the last one at the table. He was the one who served the soup, and he made a point of only serving a full ladle; he could not serve more than that, or there wouldn't be enough soup for everyone.

"Give me more soup," said the ragged boy, very dirty and

glazed-eyed. He was clearly stoned.

"I can't, buddy, there won't be enough for the others, but you already have a lot of food in there, right? There's bread, salted pie, and soup." Paul spoke quietly smiling at the boy.

All of a sudden, the young man throws the plate on the floor and grabs a knife that was at his waist and shoves it tightly into Paul's belly.

Paul let out a loud, distressing cry and everyone stopped what they're doing. The ragged boy ran away and Paul laid agonizing on the ground.

"Call an ambulance, quick." Someone was shouting from far away.

Will I die like this? Thought Paul feeling his legs and arms go numb and without resisting anymore, he loses his senses.

All his friends ran back and forth trying to help Paul at all costs.

"Let me stay with him," Wagner said terrified. "Go back to serve the people, Katy."

"OK." She said crying.

Everyone was apprehensive and began to rethink whether going there once a month was a good idea. It had already happened to other groups of people who helped. It was getting harder and harder because there was no policing on the scene, and they were at the mercy of those drugged people.

The ambulance arrived quickly, in less than eight minutes, and Paul was taken to the nearest hospital. He bled a lot and was as pale as ever.

"Dr. Taylor! Your presence is requested at the surgical

center urgently. Dr. Taylor! Your presence is requested at the surgical center urgently." Repeated the hospital operator.

Mary took the elevator and ran to the surgical center. She was already putting on her cap, gloves, and proper clothes.

"What have we got here?" she asked as she approached the man on the operating table.

"He was stabbed by a homeless man," said her assistant.

"Make sure the wound is well disinfected! These knives are dirty and crowded with bacteria. He's lost a lot of blood, right?"

"Yes. He was struck badly in the abdomen."

"Let's operate to see if his bowels were not punctured, my greatest fear," Mary said frowning.

"We're losing the patient!" cried the other doctor.

"Let's try to revive," said Mary.

She massaged Paul's heart for half an hour without stopping and asked the patient's name.

The assistant glimpsed at the file and said:

"His name is Paul."

"Come on, Paul, stay with me. It's not your turn yet, boy." She spoke softly to him. "Come on! Come on, Paul."

Mary did not give up her on patients so easily and was convinced that this would not be his time.

She continued to fight and when she had no more strength, she gave room for her colleague to continue the massage. She was exhausted.

Paul started to breathe again. Everyone sighed with relief in the operating room.

A few minutes later.

"Another cardiac arrest," said her colleague quickly.

"Let's try it again. We're not going to lose this life. Massage the heart more. Nothing was working."

"Get the defibrillator! Quick!"

Everyone was fighting and trying to save that man.

After forty-five minutes of struggle, with much effort and dedication from everyone present in the operating room, Paul started breathing again.

"Oh, thank God," Mary spoke happily and relieved.

"Thank you, guys. You guys are a fantastic team." Mary was thrilled and grateful. She wiped her forehead with her lab coat sleeve and took a deep breath.

The surgery was harder than she thought; unfortunately, the knife had pierced his bowel and the mess inside was terrible. Two doctors operated on Paul with Mary.

"You can let me take over here, Mary," her fellow surgeon said.

"OK. All that's left is to close him up. Is there anyone from the patient's family downstairs?" she asked, taking off her gloves in the other room. They were full of blood.

Yes, there is, Doctor," Patty replied.

"I'll talk to the family and be right back. They must be anxious. I want to follow this patient closely; the case was quite serious."

She went down the elevator, exhausted and still wearing a cap and surgical clothing. She'd just taken off her coat, but she was still wearing the clothes.

"Good evening! I'm Dr. Taylor. Are you related to Paul?" she asked.

"No. We're related to Andrea. Can you give us news, Doctor?"

"Sorry! My patient is someone else. I'm sure the doctor who's attending to her will come and talk to you," Mary said, reassuring the family and touching the girl's arm fondly.

She looked around and saw three distressed people. It must be those, she thought as she was going to them.

"You're Paul's relatives?" she asked looking at all three. An elegantly dressed lady, a good-looking gentleman, and another very pretty blue-eyed lady.

"Yes." The lady answered, rising quickly as the others accompanied her.

"I'm Dr. Taylor and I did his surgery. He's stable now, we'll put him into intensive care, and he is going to be under observation all night. It was a delicate surgery because the intestine was punctured, which is very bad in these cases. But we're already giving him the proper antibiotics and let's hope he recovers well."

She said everything very calmly and professionally.

"Can we see him? I am his mother," she spoke with tears in her eyes.

"Today is no longer possible. I'm going to take another look at him, and before I leave, I'll come by and give you an update, okay?"

"Is he going to be okay?" asked the distressed father.

"I hope so. We fought hard for him," Mary answered delicately.

"Thank you very much, Doctor." said the man who seemed to be the father.

"Excuse me. Rest assured, everything is going to be alright," she said with a smile, looking at his distressed mother.

"Thank you, Doctor." said the mother wiping the tears with a napkin.

Mary went up again and went straight to the ICU. She knew that the patient would already be clean and situated with all the proper equipment.

She went straight to bed seven.

She looked at Paul and recognized him immediately.

She was shocked! *Oh, my God! It's the guy who lives in the penthouse,* she noticed, puzzled. *What was it like to be stabbed by those you help? Was it a robbery?* She wouldn't know.

She checked everything, called the nurse, and prescribed all the meds for Paul.

"I hope you recover, Paul," she spoke softly to him. "Have a quiet night." she wished before leaving.

Upon her arriving at the reception, the family got up frightened.

"Please, calm down. He's all right. Currently, he is sleeping peacefully, and should there be any change, we have great doctors in the ICU.

I've prescribed pain medication every six hours, so he can have a painless night. Please, go home and rest and come back to see him tomorrow. Three people can visit with him in turns and stay with him for fifteen minutes each," she spoke quietly.

"Thank you, Doctor. I know you're doing what's best for my son."

"Does he live in the Vintage building?" She asked looking at Paul's mother.

"Yes. Do you know him?"

"I live there too, and if I'm not mistaken, we've met twice in the elevator. Only now I realized that I had seen him before. When I went back to the ICU before, I could not tell because he had oxygen on the operating table. I'm glad I could help him," she said with a smile.

"I always tell him not to go to this "soup kitchen," but there's no point in talking." She started crying again.

"Soup kitchen?" asked Mary without understanding.

"Once a month, he volunteers in a soup kitchen downtown, handing out soup and clothing to homeless people." Paul's sister said. "My name is Emily, and I am his younger sister," she said looking at Mary with her immense and beautiful blue eyes.

"Very noble, but it's really dangerous! Let's all pray for his recovery, right? Good night!"

Mary was walking away when she suddenly was hugged from behind by Paul's mother.

"Thank you, Dr. Taylor." She said touched.

"Sure! There is no need to thank me. Tomorrow, first thing, I'll come early and I'll take a look at him before anything else. Give me your phone, please, I'll let you know before the visit, which only happens at 2 p.m."

"Oh! Thank God there are angels on Earth." Paul's mother spoke already taking her business card and handing it to Mary. She took a quick look at the card and read "Social Worker."

"Don't worry, I'll call you in the morning. Have a good night." She spoke sweetly.

"Thank you so much." the three of them spoke together.

Mary knew the police had already been notified. All patients who were admitted to hospitals shot or stabbed had to report to the police. She also knew that the assailant was rarely arrested or remained in jail. That was the sad reality of big cities.

Mary left the hospital and went home thinking. *So the handsome resident of a huge penthouse volunteered in a soup kitchen?* More and more she was surprised by the world and with people thought Mary.

She could never have imagined that a man like that, well-dressed and handsome, could do charity work. Life was a box of surprises.

Mary thought he couldn't be married. Otherwise, his wife would be in the hospital too, she thought embarrassed.

He's very handsome. But I found him too conceited the first day they met, she thought to herself until she got home.

Meanwhile, at the ICU Paul was having a once-in-a-lifetime experience. He saw several people taking care of him and reassuring him that everything would be fine. They were spirits of light that helped him.

He felt grateful and comforted.

He felt God's presence there, too, and knew everything would be all right. God was giving him a new life.

He'd definitely make good use of it. He mentally thanked everyone.

The spirits left him and went around the hospital to help others who needed help.

Paul had a quiet night and slept all the time.

He woke up with a nurse by his side getting him ready for the bath, which would be right there and another already changing his bed linen.

Everything was done with haste and precision.

"Good morning!" said the nurse who was already washing him with a soft loofah.

"Good morning!" he answered weakly.

"Don't move that arm too much so the needle doesn't come out of the vein, okay?" said the other nurse.

"How did I get here?" He asked without remembering anything that had happened.

"You've been stabbed and operated on. Everything is going to be alright. Dr. Taylor is coming to see you." the nurse said quickly.

"I'm in a lot of pain here," Paul said, already reaching for his belly.

"No! No! Please, don't put your hand there. You'll feel more pain. I'm going to get you some pain killers."

The nurse left and the other one kept bathing him. The

feeling of helplessness and not being able to move was horrible because he felt a lot of pain. Being at the nurses' disposal like this, with no clothes on, was maddening. He just wanted to be at home or in the office, he thought exhausted.

He was in complete silence when the other girl arrived with a tray of syringes and came to apply the medication in the IV drip.

After a short while, he was clean, dressings made, fed a weak breakfast, and sleeping.

"How's our patient today?" asked Dr. Taylor entering the room and waking Paul up.

She was already reaching for his wrist to feel his heartbeat, examining and listening to his heart with the stethoscope. She put on a pair of gloves that had come out of her lab coat pocket and was removing the sheet to examine the bandage.

"Get the saline solution there, please." She spoke nicely to the nurse next to her.

While working focused on removing the bandage to see the state that the surgery was, she spoke softly.

"How are you feeling today, Paul?" She looked into his blue eyes and chilled. What a beautiful man! she thought.

"I'm very tired, I've never felt so weak and in so much pain," he said with his eyes closed.

"The weakness is because you've lost a lot of blood. The pains are normal, you've undergone a major surgery; the knife has hit multiple organs and it's a miracle you're here today."

He looked at the doctor for the first time.

"Do I know you?" he asked half drowsy. His voice was totally groggy.

"Yes. We live in the same building" she smiled as she spoke.

"My name is *Dr.* Taylor." She made a point of stressing that she was a dr. to keep a good distance between them.

"Oh, yes." he closed his eyes and fell asleep.

"That's right. Sleep peacefully," she said putting the bandage back on.

Paul opened his big blue eyes.

"If all goes well, tomorrow I'll discharge you from the ICU and you will be able to move on to the room," she said as she was already leaving, instructing the nurse.

Paul didn't answer anything. He was too weak and couldn't keep his eyes open. Sleeping was terrible.

"Would you like something?" asked the helpful nurse.

"Can I get up?" he asked hopefully and utterly weakened.

"No, Paul. When we're in intensive care, we don't get out of bed for anything. Do you need anything else?"

"No. Everything is fine. Thank you!" He said with a faint smile. He closed his eyes and fell asleep again.

He woke up with someone bringing a tray of food. A table was placed in front of him and the girl just smiled. Not a word was spoken.

"Could you please lift the bed up a little so I can eat?" Asked Paul to the girl from the kitchen.

"Sure!" she answered politely.

Paul managed to lift the lid and felt the yummy aroma of the food. He found out he was starving.

He ate the whole meal, with great difficulty, without being able to move much. He savored the dessert and drank all the juice. He felt much better.

After removing the empty tray and the table, the nurse came and changed the bandage. He felt a lot of pain when the wound was cleaned and asked to brush his teeth which was promptly attended to.

"Thank you very much, nurse," he said smiling at her.

Oh, my God, what a man! Thought the nurse smiling and imagining things. *He really was a treasure.*

At 2:00 p.m. sharp his mother enters the ICU.

"Oh, my son! I was so afraid! How are you, my dear?" his mother said, hugging him and kissing his pale face.

"I'm much better, Mom. Don't worry, I'll be fine."

he said reassuring his mother.

"Paul, promise me that you will quit taking part in this soup kitchen or in any other act of charity with these delinquents," his mother spoke crying.

"It's okay, Mom. I will be fine. Next time I'll go in a bulletproof vest, okay?" Paul was joking and smiling weakly.

His mother kissed him and kept running her hand through his hair.

"I love you, my son! I can't bear losing another son!" she cried sobbing.

"Calm down, Mom, I'm fine. I'll be moved to the room tomorrow and we can stay together, okay?" He said holding his mother's hand.

"Is Dad there too?" he asked, to change the subject.

"Yes. Your father and Wagner."

"So, please, go down so I can see Dad too. Please, stop crying. I'm fine." He kissed his mother's hand tenderly and closed his eyes. He hated to see his mother suffering and because of him.

His mother obeyed and went down, and his father came up to see his son.

"Paul?" called his father softly, thinking he was already asleep.

"Hi Daddy," Paul opened his eyes and a beautiful smile.

"You scared us, son" his father's eyes were filled with tears, and Paul hated himself for making his parents suffer so much.

"It's all right, Dad, don't worry. I'll be in the room tomorrow; there, we will be able to talk more."

"Are you in pain? Do you need anything?" his father asked anxiously.

"I don't need anything, Dad. Everything is fine." Paul again closed his eyes so as not to look at his father. He could not bear to see such suffering.

"Then I'm going down so your friend Wagner can come up," his father said, patting him lightly on the arm and lowering to kiss his son on the forehead.

"I love you, Daddy," Paul said emotionally.

"I love you too, son. Take care of yourself."

"You bet," replied Paul wearily.

His father left and he was waiting for Wagner for what seemed like forever.

"Hey, buddy, how are you?" Wagner asked moving closer to his friend.

"I'm in a lot of pain, man. Did they catch the kid?"

"No. He must be hiding in some abandoned building. That's to be expected, but you should worry about getting better soon, then we can do something about it."

"I'm not going to do anything, Wagner. The guy's already a junkie. He just wanted more food. He was totally whacked. Poor thing!" Paul answered.

"Wow! Man! You don't exist, you know that? Every day I spend with you I'm more surprised! You just underwent major surgery, almost died, and yet you still feel sorry for the guy?" Wagner laughed, shaking his head and admiring his friend even more.

"When I get out and I'm better, we're going to make arrangements to wear vests and stuff, okay?" he said smiling.

"Take care of yourself, brother. I have to leave; they are announcing the end of the visit. Good to see you well. Everyone sends their regards." Wagner said holding his friend's hand tightly.

Chapter Four

Wagner left work early. There would be a meeting at his children's school. After each day, he got closer and closer to them.

Thank God his children were not giving him a hard time and Mark decided to come to his senses. Wagner thought.

As he left the meeting, he ran to the hospital to pick up his friend and help him go home. Paul had been in the hospital for 20 days. He'd had a lot of visitors.

"What's up, buddy? May I come in?" said Wagner from the door of the hospital room.

"Come in, brother," Paul said, smiling at his great friend.

"It's so hot!" said Wagner holding his friend's hand affectionately. "Ready to go home?" he asked smiling.

"I'm ready to go. I'm sorry to bother you, man, but everyone seemed to have something to do, and I didn't think of anyone better," he said smiling with a lot of difficulty.

"You know you can always count on me, right?"

"Of course, buddy. Thank you very much," said Paul

leaning on Wagner and holding his belly.

"Take it easy! We have all the time in the world," Wagner said, holding his friend by the waist.

"Oh, oh, it is still very sore, man." Paul stopped and took a deep breath. "Let's take it slow. I know I can do it."

The two friends stood waiting for the hospital worker with the wheelchair that would take Paul to the hospital door.

"Are you sure you don't want to come to my house, Paul? I think you're too weak, and that's not good."

"Take me to my parents' house, man. I don't really think I can stay home alone, I'm very weak and I can't move without feeling pain."

"Of course! Let's go! It's going to be all right and in a week you're going to feel brand new."

"Good morning!" Dr. Taylor came in smiling.

"Good morning!" replied the two men together.

"How are you feeling today, Paul?" she asked looking at him.

"I'm fine, just a little pain and afraid to lift my whole body."

"There is no need to be afraid, put your spine straight, so you don't have to treat it later," she said smiling and looking at him.

"I'll keep that in mind," he said in a dry voice. "Thank you, Dr. Taylor, for all your assistance and dedication."

"Are you going to your house?" she asked as if she couldn't care less, looking at the prescription she had in her hand.

"I don't know yet, I'm thinking," Paul answered dryly.

"I'm going to take him to his parents' house, Dr. Taylor," Wagner replied politely.

"OK. I want to see you in my office in two weeks to see this bandage and the rest is all in the prescription. I want you to take a light, slow walk every day. You can't just lie around, you'll need to walk to avoid gas."

"One more thing, tomorrow you can remove your bandage and at bath time use soap on it. Dry well and there is no need to put anything on it.

The stitches have already been removed and you will get better every day. Anything you need you can call me, right?"

"And how would I do that if I don't have your cell phone number?" asked Paul sarcastically.

"I'm going to give you my card," she said politely, "you can call if you don't feel good, okay?"

"Thank you!" Paul said taking the card from her hand, without even looking at her in the face. *What a prude of a woman!* He thought upset.

Mary looked at the two of them and couldn't tell which one was more beautiful. She was delighted with such beauty of Paul and his friend.

The hospital worker arrived with the wheelchair and they went down to leave.

Just as they got in the car, Wagner said:

"What was that, brother?"

"What? I don't get it," said Paul calmly.

"The way you and the doctor treated each other, man. I swear I didn't understand anything. There was friction between you guys!" Wagner was talking and driving, not looking at Paul.

"She's my neighbor, I mean, she lives in the same building and we crossed paths twice. A pain in the ass, that's all." Paul implied that he didn't want to go on talking about that.

Wagner did not comment on anything and went to Paul's parents' house.

The days have gone by slowly. Paul worked from his home office since he was unable to go to his office. He was feeling better and better and there was no more pain.

Finally came the day of the appointment, and Wagner offered to take him to Dr. Taylor's office.

"Good morning, Dr. Taylor," Paul said as he came alone in her office.

"Good morning Paul. Sit down, please. How are you feeling?" She asked from the other side of the table without looking at him, with her eyes on the computer.

"I'm fine," he said annoyed. "Can I ask you a question?"

"Of course! That's what we are here for," she said looking at him for the first time.

He seems to look even more handsome! She thought with a poker face.

"Do you usually treat all your patients like this?"

"What do you mean, Paul? I don't understand."

"With total contempt and indifference? I came in here and you didn't even look at me in the face. You're nailed to the computer," he said annoyed.

"Excuse me? I'm not even going to answer you, you arrogant man." She was very angry with that damned conceited attitude.

"OK. Can I leave? Am I cleared to go back to work? Drive? Return to my usual activities?" He was pure ice.

"Easy there, boy! Let's take a look at this cut and I'm also going to ask for some tests to make sure everything's okay in there. Please lie down on that gurney and lift up your shirt." She spoke very seriously and professionally.

Paul got up and went to the stretcher and lay down lifting his shirt to the height of his chest.

What a beautiful, sensual body, thought Mary. She shook her head to avoid these thoughts.

"Something wrong?" Asked Paul worried.

"I'm going to squeeze a little bit in here, and you tell me if it hurts, okay?" She spoke and looked into his eyes. She felt a shiver in the back of her head and controlled herself so as not to let it show. She looked down at Paul's mouth and stopped there, longing for that beautiful, fleshy, sensual mouth.

Paul watched her eyes in his mouth and looked at that beautiful doctor for the first time.

Thick eyebrows, fleshy and sexy mouth, beautiful eyes. He immediately felt a desire to touch her and make love to her.

His breathing got faster and he got an erection, which didn't go unnoticed by the doctor who gave him an angry look.

"Sorry!" Paul said embarrassed, looking away. Mary said nothing and passed her hand on Paul's chest, which was much worse because the desire between them increased greatly.

Paul looked at her fascinated, *what a beautiful woman!*

Mary gently lowered her hand to the scar and groped it gently, squeezing slowly and imagining her body next to Paul's. She made circular movements and he was getting more and more aroused. They both looked at each other and Paul sat on the stretcher facing Mary, who was paralyzed with desire.

They looked deeply at each other. She slowly approached him, always looking into his eyes, their bodies almost touching each other so intense was their desire.

A desire to kiss, embrace that manly and beautiful body, desire to rub in the middle of his legs.

They remained as immobile as possible, facing each other with lust and desire.

Slowly he took her hand, she felt a shiver go through her spine and there was a throbbing pain in her uterus.

He came closer, staring at her intensely and she knew she would not resist. She looked into his face with adoration, every part of it, until she fixated on his mouth. Without thinking of anything, she opened her lips inviting Paul for a kiss. She slowly approached and touched her lips on his, introduced her tongue, slowly exploring his entire mouth, sucking affectionately, slowly; it was an intense kiss, sensual, wet, and full of lust. He hugged her by the waist, descending a little from the stretcher until he was just leaning against her. His hand went down to her ass, squeezing her body against his so that she could fit between his legs. She felt the hard and large limb and touched it, without any shame and unreservedly. They kept exploring each other's lips, kissing and kissing more and more. He panted and moaned softly. She was eager to have him all there just to herself.

He stopped kissing her mouth and moved to her neck licking, biting and sucking, moaning more and more, taken by desire, moved his mouth up to her ear and said in a hoarse voice.

"Mary! You make me crazy, full of sinful desires and thoughts. You are so hot!" As he spoke in her ear, she became delirious and moaned madly.

Their bodies were so united that it would be impossible to pass anything between them.

Suddenly, she came to reason and she walked away shaky and disheveled. The two of them had a heavy, out-of-control breath, they looked into each other's eyes, and she felt all her love for that man.

"Oh my God!" She said passing her hands through her messy hair and moving away. "Sorry, Paul! I really don't know what happened." She was super embarrassed and he didn't know what to say.

"Let's just calm down, okay?" he spoke softly.

"Yes. Sure! God in heaven! What happened here should never have happened, Paul. I'm so sorry." She stared at him nervously.

"All right, let's continue our consultation and forget about it." He wouldn't stop talking and blushed.

"OK. You can go back to work and you won't be able to carry weight for six months. If you feel any pain or fever, please come to me. Here's your prescription; in case you feel pain, you can take these," she said without looking at him. "Do these exams when you feel better. They're not urgent. Follow-up only."

"Thank you very much!" He got up and went to the door, put his hand on the doorknob, and stopped." He spent a few seconds with his hand there, undecided whether to go out or look at her again. He opened the door and left.

Mary, who was holding her breath, leaned back in her chair and sighed in relief. She sat down and closed her eyes, put her hand on her forehead, and began to go through that moment one more time...

"Are you okay?" Her secretary came in and she didn't even listen. Mary was startled and nearly fell off her chair.

"Jesus, Darah, please knock!" she said annoyed.

"I'm sorry, Dr. Taylor," she said embarrassed.

"All right." She said impatiently. "Do I have any more patients, or was this one the last?" She asked Darah. She was tired, sweaty, and wanted to go home.

"You still have two more patients, but both are to show post-op scans; it will be quick." She said with professionalism.

"You can send them in, please."

"Yes, ma'am."

"And Darah," called Mary.

"Yes."

"Sorry! I'm very tired today. I barely slept last night and I still have three surgeries after lunch."

"It's all right, Dr. Taylor, don't worry," she said politely.

After seeing the two patients, Mary said goodbye to her secretary and went home to take a shower. She usually didn't do that. From the office, she would go to the hospital to have lunch and spend the rest of the day there. But today, it was different, she thought as she was driving home. She wanted some time for herself. Even if it was half an hour, she needed to think.

Chapter Five

Paul looked angry and Wagner didn't say a word. They both went quietly to Paul's mother's house.

"Wagner?" said Paul in a low voice. "I'm going to bother you one more time, buddy."

"Sure! Anything," said his friend smiling.

"I'm going to go get my stuff and you drop me off at home? Mom and Dad aren't here; it'll be easier to sneak away," he said with a smile too.

"Right! I'll come there to give you a hand."

"OK. Thank you very much, my friend."

"Don't mention it! It's a pleasure to help you."

The two friends got in Paul's parents' house and went straight to his room.

Paul collected all his things and called the maid to say that he was already leaving and that everything was fine.

The girl wished him good luck and the two of them walked out the door.

Paul wanted to be alone and think. He really needed to

think a lot.

"Is everything all right, man?" Wagner asked thinking Paul was very thoughtful.

"I'm fine. Mary said I can drive, work, everything... I just can't carry heavy items, but I'm fine."

"Mary, huh?" said his friend mocking and smiling.

"Oh, man, stop it! I didn't even notice I said the name instead of Doctor." Paul was smiling and relaxed.

"Did you at least have the decency to notice how hot the doctor is?" said Wagner licking his lips and laughing.

"Man! Come on! Stop being a pervert!" They both laughed and Paul put his hand on his belly feeling the stitches.

"Are you all right?" Asked Wagner worried.

"It's all right, yes," he said looking at his smiling friend.

"Are you sure you're not hiding something from me?"

"Oh man, you won't let it go, will you?" he laughs.

"OK. Then, it's fine. Anything you need, you call me,"

"You can count on it. Thank you very much."

Wagner helped Paul take his stuff home, sat his friend comfortably in an armchair, gave him control of the TV, and went home.

As soon as Wagner left, Paul leaned his head against the back of the armchair and closed his eyes.

He went over his and Mary's kiss countless times and went crazy with desire for that woman.

How in the name of God have they come to that point?

Paul was distressed and wanted at all costs to call Mary and ask her to come to his penthouse later in the night.

I need her, he thought incredulously. *Oh, my God, I need her!* He couldn't believe what he was thinking or feeling.

Mary took a very cold bath and lay on her bed. She wanted to think for half an hour. That was the limit she could stay there, that she could afford to think of Paul.

Oh my God! How indecent, how unethical of me! She thought, sad. Never! Never! In all her life as a doctor, she had been involved with any patient. She always sought to be professional and did not even want to think about the tragedy that would be if someone found out.

She simply almost ate the man. *What a hot man, what a mouth, what a body! Oh, I can't think of him and the worst, I could come face to face with him at any moment.*

She closed her eyes and just for remembering him, she longed to kiss him.

That man will destroy my life, she thought as she got up fast. She had to have lunch before the surgeries, and she was late. As she was going to the surgical center, Mary decided that she would erase any trace of Paul from her mind.

And that's how it was for two weeks. No sinful thoughts or of orgies in bed. No sex and a fleshy, sexy mouth.

A month later, Mary no longer remembered that Paul existed and Paul resumed his hectic life as a lawyer, without even remembering Dr. Taylor.

He'd done all the tests, but he didn't want to take them

to her. Things were good without seeing her.

It had been a long day, and Paul was dying to take a shower and relax at home.

He took the elevator, pressed penthouse and it barely started going up when it stopped on the next floor, the garage. He simply closed his eyes; he was tired.

"Good evening!" He heard Dr. Taylor's voice getting into the elevator with him.

"Good evening!" He answered looking at her ass.

What a gorgeous woman! May God give me strength, he thought.

"Paul."

When she turned around, he was already grabbing her face with both hands, sticking his hands into her black straight hair and pulling her head to meet his. Their mouths joined in a passionate and delicate kiss. He kissed her as if there were nothing but two souls.

He pulled her away a little and said in a hoarse voice and full of desire.

"I want you so much! Oh, my God, you are too beautiful!" He kept kissing her mouth and talking, "you're really hot!" He placed his lips upon hers and kissed, his tongue searched with anxiety and desire.

Mary's body was all soft and shaking; she'd even forgotten to breathe.

They looked at each other's eyes, and Mary felt her eyes darken with desire.

"Come here!" He said softly and clouded by emotion. He pressed the penthouse floor button.

He hugged her placing his hands on her back and moaning. Not resisting any longer, Mary leaned over. The chemistry was too intense, they were very excited and he kept kissing her with passion and desire.

"I need you, please I can't hold my desire for you anymore. That was all I thought about all these days, wanting you every second."

"Let's go then," she said trembling.

The entire time he looked at her with his blue eyes.

They got off the elevator. They completely forgot about the cameras.

"I need to open the door," he said between a kiss and another.

He just got away for the time necessary so that he could use his key to open the door and they went upstairs with a mad urgency.

The room was half lit; there was only a lamp. They kissed standing until he lifted her up and she spread her legs, crossing them at his waist. He carried her to bed, always with his lips on her mouth.

They were panting when he lay on top of her, covering her whole with his firm, manly body.

He stopped kissing her, rolled to the side and started taking off his shirt; that was all very sexy. His chest was firm and manly and with chiseled abs. At the same time, Mary got more excited than ever and looked fascinated at the body of that Greek god.

He threw his shirt aside and came near her and took her in his arms.

"How soft you are! I'm crazy about you." Paul spoke, already pulling Mary's blouse up and taking off everything else.

"Come here," Mary called him softly. She hugged him and was caressing the back of his head very slowly and with her other hand on his back. He shivered all over with the touch of her hand.

Paul moaned with pleasure.

He lifted her by the hip and pulled her closer to him. He stroked her thighs and went up and down kissing her the entire time. His tongue moved slowly through every little bit of her body; she was ready.

Gently he was lowering her panties and she helped him by lifting one leg and then the other. Then he moved up his hand and unbuttoned her bra, discarding the articles away from them.

They were now both naked and completely exposed to each other.

He moaned and so did she.

He stretched out his hand to the bed table, took a condom, and opened it with his teeth. He put it on fast and with experience and she opened more for him and pulled him closer with her legs. He penetrated her deep and stopped, looked at her and said in a hoarse, low voice:

"Look at me, baby, in my eyes... I want to hear you say

my name."

Mary repeated his name until they were both satisfied.

It was amazing! It was beautiful!

Exhausted with passion and desire, they rolled on the bed and he took off the used condom, putting it in the wastebasket next to the bed.

Without thinking twice, he took her in his arms and brought her close to him, involving her waist, kissing and smelling the scent of her hair. She was sleepy and so was he. They spooned quiet and lost in their thoughts.

They didn't say anything to each other, and it was just wonderful. Suddenly he spoke softly:

"You're beautiful and everything I imagined..."

She took a deep breath and said softly. "I loved every second... your affection and care."

"Honey, it couldn't be any different. I dreamed about it. I fantasized every second of it."

She was super moved and took shelter even more in his arms and thought how easy it would be to be madly in love with that caring man. It was all a woman wanted and could wish for: a love for life.

Chapter Six

Mary woke up scared and looked to the side. She saw Paul sleeping very calmly. She looked at him and felt she needed to get away from that man before she could suffer. He was very engaging and the passion between them was like fire.

Every time they met, they already wanted to attack each other. This was dangerous and Mary didn't want any complications in her life. Things were good as they were, and she didn't have time for it.

She got up slowly and took her clothes scattered around the beautiful room and went to change in the bathroom. She'd get out of there as fast as she could.

She wouldn't want to face Paul's eyes and she was afraid of having another relapse and letting herself be carried away by desire and passion.

She closed the door and took the elevator to her floor. It was 11:00 p.m., and she needed a bath, food, and bed.

She took a warm and relaxing shower, heated up the food in the microwave and ate on her lap out on her balcony while looking at the moon. Tomorrow would be a new day.

She brushed her teeth and went to bed. The moment she put her head on the pillow, she was already fast asleep.

Paul woke up and noticed that it was already 2:00 in the morning and that he was completely alone.

"She left for her apartment," implied Paul.

He decided to get up and take a quick shower. He needed to talk to Mary about this crazy attraction that existed between them, he thought.

They never talked about it. They just had sex. "That wasn't normal," Paul considered.

After the shower, he went to the huge balcony and sat in a modern rocking chair. He stayed there a long time reflecting and still feeling all the energy in his body.

"Tomorrow, I will speak to her." He thought resolutely. He went to bed and it took him a while to fall asleep.

Mary arrived at the hospital on time at 6:00 a.m. She needed to make rounds to check on her patients before she went to her office.

She slept very little, woke up several times in the middle of the night always thinking about Paul. She'd have to put an end to it for the sake of both of them.

At 7:45 a.m., she was ready to leave the hospital and go to her office when her assistant came running towards her.

"Dr. Taylor," called Patty.

"Yes, any problems with one of my patients?" She asked worriedly.

"No, doctor, everything is fine. Dr. Moses wants to see you. He is waiting for you in his office," she said politely.

Mary thanked her and went to the office of the hospital director and majority owner.

Knock. Knock. Knock.

"Come in," the doctor answered, taking off his reading glasses.

"Good morning!" Greeted Mary politely.

"Good morning, darling!" Answered the doctor, who was at least thirty years older than Mary.

"You wanted to see me, Moses?" She spoke sweetly.

"Yes." I need a big favor, and I hope you can help me.

"Sure! Is there something wrong?" Her voice showed concern.

"Mary, I need you in New York today." He said staring at her.

"But what happened?"

"Sissy went to New York to do some shopping and strolling, but she slipped and fell while on a ramp and was taken to Mount Sinai. Because she was feeling a lot of pain on her right side," he continued, "an MRI was done, and an orange-sized tumor was found on her liver."

"Oh my God!" Mary was shocked.

"The doctors want to operate today, and I need someone I trust there to help with the surgery and to be by her side. I'd go myself, but you know how the hospital's here. I can't leave now."

Sissy had been Moses' wife for forty years and their love was the most beautiful thing Mary had ever seen. She regarded the two as if they were her parents, and Mary could never refuse a request like that.

"When do you want me to go?" Mary asked him.

"Now, darling." He said apprehensively.

"OK. I'm going to ask a colleague to take over my entire schedule."

"Will I go on your private plane?" She asked and was already getting up to leave.

"Yes. It'll be ready in two hours. This will give you time to pack your bag and make other arrangements."

"Everything will be all right, Moses." Mary went around the table and gave him a loving hug.

"Yes." He said with a choking voice. "Mary?" He called her moved, "take care of my Sissy, please," and began to cry.

Mary couldn't resist and her eyes were full of tears. "Of course! Don't worry, I'll stay for as long as it takes."

Mary left the office in a hurry and made all the necessary arrangements for her departure to New York from inside the car.

She left instructions with her two colleagues that would replace her in surgeries, hospital rounds, and at her office. Everything was resolved so that nothing could go wrong and she could be in New York and not worry about having to come back.

She parked in the garage and called the elevator while she called her mother and warned her of the unexpected trip. She asked her mother to tell the cleaning lady not to make food because she wouldn't be home.

After everything was all set up, she packed her suitcase, took off her hospital clothes, took another quick shower, and went to the airport by taxi. She didn't want to waste time looking for a parking space for her own car.

She arrived at the airport ten minutes before the two-hour deadline. She identified herself and walked in.

Twenty minutes later, she was already comfortably seated on Dr. Moses' private plane.

The flight attendant asked if she'd like anything and she said no.

The weather forecast in New York was cold and she was prepared for it.

The flight was quiet, and all Mary could do was think of Paul. She decided she wouldn't call him to report her trip.

I don't owe him anything, she thought quietly.

She arrived in New York and she could feel the power of that city. Monumental and noble.

She thanked the crew members, took a taxi, and ran to the hotel that her secretary had already booked for her.

She changed her clothes and went to the hospital. She didn't even remember to eat.

The surgery was scheduled to begin in two hours because all the surgical centers of the hospital were taken.

Mary had a long conversation with the two surgeons. She saw and reviewed the tests done and was really worried.

The tumor was large, and it was going to be a difficult and dangerous surgery. She left the meeting with the doctors and went to the restaurant of the hospital, ate something, and called Moses.

While waiting for her food, she reflected on life and how

short it was and how fast it went.

Her phone rang and she answered.

"Hello!"

"It's me, Mary!" said the anxious doctor. "I've seen Sissy, and she's fine. We're doing the surgery in two hours. Don't worry Moses, I'll be with her all the time."

"Thank you, Mary!" he said moved.

"Don't mention it. I'll stay in touch with you. I'll call you as soon as I finish the surgery, okay?" she said goodbye quickly as her food had arrived.

As she ate the first bite, her phone rang again and as it was an unknown number, she decided not to answer. She was hungry and she wasn't going to solve anything over the phone with anyone. All instructions on patients and surgeries were with her secretary and nothing could be done from afar.

She decided to turn off her cell phone so she could eat quietly.

Paul insisted three more times on Mary's cell phone and every time, it went to voicemail.

I'll leave to speak to her personally. I'm going to your apartment today, he decided turning off his cell phone.

Mary went to the O.R. as soon as she was called. She put her things and clothes in a locker and changed her clothes. The operating room was very modern and with lots of new and recent equipment.

The two colleagues arrived and the three of them talked about the intervention they were going to make. Everyone gave their opinions and reached a consensus.

Sissy arrived calm and sleepy. They had already given her a tranquilizer to be very relaxed.

"It's going to be okay, my dear." She took Sissy's hand and gave a sweet smile.

"Thank you, Mary, for being here with me," she said drowsily.

The anesthesiologist came and they started the surgery that would last seven hours.

It was harder than they expected, and Sissy would be left with a drain for at least two weeks. She wouldn't be able to go home any time soon. She'd start chemo soon and continue treatment in her town. They were hopeful and with great expectations of improvement.

Mary went to the hotel quickly, took a shower and went back to the hospital. She was going to spend the night with Sissy. She talked with Moses for over an hour and when Sissy went to the semi-ICU room, Mary took a picture of her, still drowsy to show him. He cried and Mary cried too. She promised to put her on video as soon as she woke up, no matter the time. But they both knew Sissy would sleep all night.

The nurse assured her that she could sleep in peace, that she would enter the room every forty minutes. Mary thanked her and praised God for sending angels into her life. She'd been on call since 6:00 a.m. She was so tired she couldn't take it anymore. The surgery had taken too long, and she was exhausted.

Mary got comfortable on the sofa bed and fell asleep. She

didn't check any messages on her cell phone.

Both Mary and Sissy had a good night. All the drugs were given so that Sissy would not feel any pain and so it was.

The next day she was fine and with a heartier face, which was a real miracle.

Chapter Seven

Wagner felt lonely and frustrated. He didn't have the energy to go out and go to nightclubs and bars to find a mate. He didn't like dating sites and didn't know how to date anymore.

After so many years of marriage and living comfortably and happily, he really was in dire straits, he thought smiling.

He decided he'd call his roommate and Paul's friend.

"Hello." answered a jovial voice.

"Debby?" He asked a bit awkwardly.

"Yes. Who is it?"

"This is Wagner, Paul's friend. Do you remember me?" He asked, and at the same time, he hated himself for having called.

"Hi, how are you? Wow! It's been a while since we last spoke, huh?" She spoke smiling and very friendly.

"Indeed." He said embarrassed.

"Is everything all right, Wagner?" She seemed worried.

"Everything is fine. Listen, Debby," Wagner coughed nervously, "I'm sorry I'm calling you..." He stuttered a little, "I was going to ask you out for a drink or dinner. What do you think?" He said it and held his breath.

"I think it's a great idea! I really need to relax a little. When were you thinking?"

"It's up to you."

"Let me see here; I'm free today, tomorrow, and on Friday."

"How about today? I can pick you up at home, so we'll can go in one car." He said quickly.

"Great! It's done. "I'll text you the address and location, all right?"

"Yes."

"OK, then. See you later, bye.

"Bye."

"Oh! I almost forgot," he said with a smile. "What time?"

"Does 8:00 o'clock work for you?"

"Great, Wagner, how about dinner?"

"Good. Do you have a restaurant in mind?" He asked politely.

"No, dear, everything for me is fine. I love food," she laughed, and so did he.

They said goodbye and Wagner relaxed. He was apprehensive and nervous, but she was fun and friendly.

At 8:00 p.m. sharp, Wagner rang Debby's apartment intercom.

"I'm just coming down," she replied pantingly.

"OK." Replied Wagner cheerfully. Debby was gorgeous!

"You look beautiful," Wagner said as he kissed her cheek.

"Hi!" She answered kissing him back and smiling.

"Where do you want to go?" asked Wagner politely.

"My dear, I love food, so it can be in a cozy place without much noise. How about that?"

"Great! I have the perfect place for us."

The two came out smiling and cheerful. Wagner and Debby were having fun and were loving getting to know each other better.

The days flew by and which turned into months.

They'd been going out for two months and the two of them were getting along and laughed at each other's jokes. Debby was sweet, intelligent, beautiful, fun, and very competent.

"Being with you, I don't need to bother Paul," Wagner said biting his sandwich and laughing.

Debby laughed and punched his strong, muscular arm.

It was the first time Wagner was going out with anyone after his wife died. But life went on and he missed having someone in his life. He already knew Debby from parties where he and Paul went together, and one thing led to another and they were loving that their involvement was hot and without much pressure. Things between the two were light and smooth.

"Debby, how about we arrange for us to have lunch at my place? The kids want to meet you." He said with a smile.

He was tired of having to meet her only in public places or at her house, like now.

"I don't know, Wagner, you think they're going to like me?" she asked apprehensively.

"Of course, love! Whoever doesn't like you is crazy. But only I can love you." He was stopped with what he was doing and started looking at her intensely.

"Oh! My love! How beautiful! You're a very beautiful man indeed."

"I know." He said smiling.

"You're very cocky, you know."

"Come here, baby," Wagner called by opening his arms to her.

"Yes." She cuddled up to that tall, manly man and loved to be embraced by those arms that conveyed safety and confidence.

"Debby, I know it's hard for you to start a life with my baggage." He smiled awkwardly. "But I never thought I'd be able to love again."

Debby looked at him affectionately and kissed his mouth. It was a wet and sensual kiss and she really wanted to make him happy.

"Wagner, I love you, and if I have to start my life with an entire army..." the two laughed loudly. "Then I think I do want to have that lunch."

"Oh, my love! You've made me the happiest man in the world and to prove it, I will love you like never before."

Wagner took Debby off the floor, took her to the bedroom, and lay her in bed. There was intense chemistry between the two of them and they loved each other like never before. Wagner loved Debby with the soul, their bodies came together as if they were just one, and Debby knew Wagner would love her forever.

"Family gathering, folks!" Wagner called the children who were all in the room playing video game.

No one paid attention. They were all in the middle of a competition and it was the last stage.

Wagner came into the room and said:

"Did you hear that?" He spoke a little louder.

"Just a moment, Dad, we're almost done here. We'll be there in a minute!"

Wagner returned to the kitchen and continued to make dinner. The best time for them to talk, he thought. Everyone was relaxed and it would be the perfect time to talk about Debby. He was apprehensive whether his children would accept the fact that he was dating. He loved Debby and wanted her as his wife.

"I won! I won!" Cried Mark.

The children laughed and it was the best sound Wagner could hear. After all the suffering, the laughter and jokes came back.

"So, what is it, daddy?" said Cinthia.

"Let's sit down for dinner and we'll talk," said a nervous Wagner.

When everyone was already eating and talking at the same time, Wagner said:

"I'm dating, and I wanted to know from you how you feel about meeting my new love."

"You what dad?" Mark asked smiling.

"I want you to know that no one will ever replace your

mother." Everyone stared at him without saying anything and Wagner was getting more and more nervous.

"So..." he cleared his throat twice. "I thought I'd invite her for lunch here next Sunday and introduce her to you. Is it all right?"

The children didn't say anything, looking seriously at him.

Wagner shifted in the chair. He was uncomfortable with the looks of his children and the silence was absolute.

"Guys, say something." Their dad sweated and trembled.

"CONGRATULATIONS, DAD!" the three shouted clapping, they laughed and rose to hug the father who wept like a baby.

"Daddy..." said the youngest daughter, Ana. "Finally!" Everyone laughed and kissed their father on the head, passing their hands and messing Wagner's hair.

He sighed with relief and hugged his children.

Thank you, God.

That day Wagner went to bed thanking the universe for everything. Mark had actually kept the promise he made at the police station. He had never got involved in fights again. He was dedicating himself to his studies and wanted to do an internship at one of Wagner's companies. He wanted to start work early.

Wagner was proud and happy for his son.

The big day arrived and he called Paul to go too. He felt awkward introducing Debby.

"This is my girlfriend, Debby," Wagner spoke apprehensively to his three children, who smiled at his nervousness.

"Hi, Debby!" The three of them spoke, smiling and looking at that beautiful woman.

"Hi!" She said smiling too and feeling a little awkwardly in front of the children.

"Come and see the house, Debby," said Cinthia, the middle daughter taking Debby by the hand. Mark started talking to talk to Paul and Ana went after Debby.

"Excuse me, uncle Paul, I'm going to play a game. Daddy, if you need any help with the barbecue, just call me," said a quiet and peaceful Mark.

"Hey, man? Are you okay?" asked Paul putting his hand on Wagner's shoulder.

"I was so nervous," he spoke smiling and already putting on his barbecue apron.

"Debby is wonderful, Wagner. It's going to be all right." Paul said calmly.

"You look so down. If you need to talk, we can have a beer later." Wagner offered to do it because he thought his friend wasn't ok.

"It's all right, just tired." He gave a faint smile.

Paul walked away from his friend and sat in a rocking chair facing the pool. The weather was great and he thought of Mary.

It's been two weeks. He hasn't heard from her since that wild night. She hasn't answered her cell phone or answered the doorbell, and the only news he got at the hospital was that she was traveling.

"I can't tell you where she is," the secretary repeated for

the third time Paul called.

The feeling he had was that Mary had disappeared on purpose not to face him.

Chapter Eight

Every day that went by, Sissy got stronger and better. Moses had already gone to visit his wife twice and wanted her back home. After discussing the matter over with the doctors and Mary promising that she would always be there, the doctors discharged Sissy and they could return home.

Chemotherapy was working and the doctors were impressed by the strength and will to live of that 56-year-old lady.

Sissy's love of life was something that surprised everyone, including Mary.

"Happy to go back home, honey?" Asked Mary delicately.

"Very happy and grateful to all of you, especially you dear Mary." She spoke holding Mary's hands and filling her eyes with tears.

"You don't have to thank me, I do it from the heart. You know how much I love you two, don't you?"

"Oh, yes, darling. You're a real daughter. The daughter Moses and I didn't have. Thank you!"

"I'm the one who's grateful, Sissy, for having you in my

life and seeing your willpower in living. I'm learning a lot from you. Your effort is astounding," Mary said moved.

"Dear Mary, I see you never loved, am I right?" She asked raising an eyebrow at Mary.

"You mean the love between a man and a woman? I don't think so, Sissy." Mary replied with a smile.

"Yes. Yes. That's the love I'm talking about." She replied.

"That love I really don't know and I'll even confess to you." She said looking into Sissy's eyes. "I think I'm afraid." She laughed timidly.

"Mary, don't be afraid to love and devote yourself to that love. Love is beautiful and it can work. I don't really fight for myself, honey. I fight for Moses." She said holding Mary's hand fondly.

"What do you mean?"

"How could I leave and let my Moses here? Never! He wouldn't last a month without me. That Mary is love! You think of the other before yourself. May even be very presumptuous of me, but I know my Moses."

"Yes, Sissy, he really loves you so much," Mary said.

"I met someone, Sissy, but I don't know if it's love."

"Really? Tell me everything," said Sissy straightening in the chair getting ready to hear her sweet Mary.

"There's nothing much. We just have an overwhelming fire. We can't take our hands off each other, and I'm finding it all very strange and new."

"Do you love him?" Asked Sissy looking into Mary's eyes.

"I think so, but what if he just wants casual sex? I don't want to be just one more in his bed," she lowered her head sadly.

"I think you're going to have to figure out what you two really want. It is very important that you have good chemistry in bed."

Before Mary could answer, the hotel phone rang and she was told the car that would drop them off at the airport.

"We're just coming down," Mary replied to the receptionist.

"Let's go?" she called affectionately, taking the luggage of the two and putting them in the hotel cart.

Mary helped Sissy and they went to their destination.

Paul once again went to Mary's apartment and insistently rang the bell.

This is very strange, he thought upset.

Today was kitchen soup day and he wouldn't let himself be overwhelmed. He asked his assistant to buy a knife-proof vest and he would participate for sure.

"Are you sure you want to volunteer, man?" Wagner asked worriedly.

"Of course, I'm sure. It's all right. Let's go?" He spoke excitedly and happy to be active again.

The place where the homeless were staying was very crowded and they were all afraid the food was not going to be enough. Once again, there would be confusion.

Thanks to Paul's father, who had friends in the other law enforcement agencies, some police officers were assigned

to secure the place. Anything suspicious and the police would act. Everything went well and everyone was fed and happy.

Paul got home around 9:30 p.m. He took a shower and sat down to have some wine on the balcony. The moon was full and huge and he gazed at it for several long, beautiful minutes.

Suddenly, he heard the bell ring and wondered if it was Wagner, the only person who entered his building unannounced.

He was just wearing boxers and didn't mind answering the door like that. It was hot and his friend wouldn't mind.

He opened the door and got the biggest scare. In a little blue dress, short and very loose, was Dr. Taylor.

"Hi." She said awkwardly, looking at him from top to bottom. "Is it a bad time? Sorry to come unannounced, I arrived today from New York."

"Hi." said a gaped Paul.

"Can I come in, or are we going to stand at the door talking?" She said with a half-smile.

"Yes. Sure! Come in. I'm just going to put on some shorts. Make yourself at home," he spoke and was already going up the stairs, letting her close the door herself.

She was beautiful! My God, I ask for strength in the face of this temptation, Paul prayed not too confidently.

He put on tight shorts, which made him even sexier and went down the stairs barefoot.

Mary was on the balcony admiring the view and looking at the moon in front of her. Wonderful and beautiful, she thought with a sigh.

"Beautiful, isn't it? The moon," he said behind her.

"Yes..." She spoke softly.

She turned around and he was facing her now. They were very close together.

"Ahem." She cleared her throat and asked if she could sit down.

"I'll get my glass of wine. Would you like some? I just poured it," he said pointing to the charming little table next to the rocking chair.

"Yes, please. Thank you!" she replied sweetly.

He ran into the room and took the wine bottle and the glass. He filled it to half and offered it to her. Their fingers touched and she chilled with desire.

"Paul, we need to talk," she said softly and had a sip of wine.

"I think so too." He said while drinking his wine.

"You've disappeared without a trace. Do you usually do this and leave your patients without any assistance?" He asked ironically.

"As far as I know, I haven't left anyone without assistance. There were three doctors replacing me. Did you need me?" She asked. She wasn't going to let that spoiled guy talk to her like that at all.

If I needed you? Thought Paul staring at her. *I was CRAZY about you.*

"No, I didn't need you." He answered by taking another sip of the wine and filling their glasses again.

"Are you trying to get me drunk?" She asked looking at him with an ugly face.

"Are you going to let your guard down or not? It's impossible to talk like that," he said upset.

"Yes, I really screwed up coming here" She stood up all of a sudden and turned to him and said, "I'm out."

Before she crossed the balcony into the room, he gently grabbed her arm and spoke softly.

"I'm sorry, Mary, can we start over?" He said, letting go of her arm for fear of not resisting that beautiful, tender skin.

"All right." She said looking into his eyes.

"Would you rather sit here on the balcony or in the living room?" He asked politely.

"Where would you like to sit?" She said smiling.

She is so beautiful! He thought looking at her mouth and lowering his eyes to the small neckline of her breasts.

"I prefer the balcony. I was here when you arrived."

"Do you have cheese?" She asked all of a sudden. "I love cheese and wine."

"I don't. I'm sorry." He said awkwardly.

"I've some. How about we grab this bottle and we go have this conversation in my apartment? I have cheese and you have the wine. Perfect combination."

"Yes, we can. Just a moment, I'm going to put on a T-shirt."

"Please don't put on anything too tight. Those shorts are enough." She laughed with her mouth and eyes and Paul had never seen her so beautiful and relaxed.

"You got it!" He said smiling and running up the stairs.

He put on the first t-shirt he came across and put on a pair of comfortable slippers.

She was in the same place admiring the moon. He made no noise and was admiring her back, her straight, very black, loose hair and that ass! That was really a masterpiece.

"Let's go?" He said as if he had just arrived. She turned around smiling and they went to her apartment.

They got in the elevator and smiled at each other; they were both remembering the last time they were alone together here.

"Did you know there are cameras here?" She said, blushing and looking at the camera. "We forgot it," she said with a smile.

"That's true," the doorman must have enjoyed our show. They both laughed and left the elevator.

It was easy for Mary to open the door this time since she had the whole lock changed. She didn't like anything broken.

"Make yourself comfortable," She said opening the door for him. "I'll go to the kitchen and get the cheese."

"I'll accompany you." He said with the bottle in his hand.

"Over here then." She said cheerfully.

"Could you get the glasses, please? They are over there in the corner cabinet. I'm going to open the cheese."

Quickly and masterfully, she opened the cheese, cut it and put it on the board.

"Should we stay on the balcony or in the living room?" She asked with the board in her hand.

"What do you think?" he asked smiling.

"We can stay on the balcony. I have a sofa where we can sit, talk and have this wonderful wine together with this delicious cheese."

They settled comfortably on the sofa and ate the delicious Swiss cheese.

"Wonderful, Mary!" He said while eating. "I've suddenly realized I was hungry." He said.

"A delight indeed. I cared for a patient from Switzerland a few years ago who was here on vacation and he was so grateful that he sends me cheese from time to time. I love it!"

"Why did you disappear?" He asked suddenly.

"Who said I disappeared? I went to New York and left three colleagues here to replace me."

"What was so important that you couldn't say goodbye?" He was jealous of her.

"I didn't know I needed to say goodbye and ask your permission, Paul." She was very firm yet polite and delicate.

"Sorry! You really don't have to."

"Still, I'm going to tell you, not because I owe you any explanation, but because I want to." She made it very clear.

"There's no need to explain. It's none of my business." He said firmly.

"Paul... Listen, please, we're here to talk and not to fight, right?"

I'm here to LOVE you!

"OK. Sure." He said, drinking more wine.

"I went to New York because a good friend who was spending some time there fell and got hurt, and when she was admitted to the hospital, they discovered a large tumor in her liver. I went there to help with the surgery and I was with her all this time." Mary spoke quietly and sweetly, and Paul loved her even more.

"I'm sorry, Mary." He said politely. "I thought you were running away from me after what happened between us."

"I want you to know something about me Paul, I never run away from anything." She got up and went to the edge of the balcony and put both elbows on the handrails.

He got up and stood behind her, dying to kiss her. He got a little closer to her and smelled her hair. She felt it from behind and leaned against his chest. Without resisting any longer, Paul hugged her waist bringing her very close to him and began kissing and sniffing her neck. The feeling of being with her back to him and being embraced like this was wonderful. She was so slender and beautiful that he hugged her with both arms and kissed her head and her neck, kissing and sucking gently to leave no marks.

They were already super excited and Paul moved down both hands passing them on her thighs up and down, suspending the dress and passing his hands on her legs and teasing her.

She turned to hug him by the neck. Before that, she let the straps of the little dress loosen and all that was left were her tiny panties and her bare breasts.

"You want to make me crazy, Mary?" He asked full of desire kissing and sucking her mouth, passing his hands on her firm and bulky breasts.

His shorts were about to burst and Mary brought them

down so he had nothing underneath. Impatient, Paul took off his shirt and watch and threw them aside, not caring about anything else.

Mary was beautiful, hot and sexy, and he knew he couldn't get away from her. He was desperately in love, he thought, sucking her mouth with passion.

They made love right there on the big couch on the balcony and since Paul wasn't wearing a condom, it was the greatest delight in the world.

Feeling Mary that way was the best feeling ever and he hugged and kissed her endlessly, even after they had completely satisfied themselves. He just couldn't take his lips off Mary and he started kissing her all over again until they made love once again.

Paul was worn out and satisfied as ever. Mary was his great love.

Chapter Nine

Mary felt she needed to stop it all. It couldn't be that whenever they were close to each other, they ended up in bed.

She moved to get up and Paul held her by the waist.

"Stay here." He said affectionately kissing her head and smelling her hair. He ran his chin through her head and said a little sleepy:

"You're so sweet," he smiled with his eyes closed.

"Paul, we need to talk. This is not right. Every time we meet, it ends like this, it's all about sex." She said seriously.

Paul let Mary go at once and sat on the big couch.

"You think this is just sex? For you what we have is just sex? I'm sorry, dear! I think I've heard enough of you." He said dryly.

Without giving further explanations, he took his clothes and got dressed quickly.

"Wait, Paul, let's talk." She insisted, putting on the dress fast.

"I think you've said it all. Good night!"

He left angry and didn't look back. In the rush of leaving he forgot his slippers and watch at Mary's house. He shrugged and didn't give it a second thought. He had more watches and slippers at home. He no longer wanted to see Mary, she was a person without feelings and he wouldn't admit that she mocked him.

He loved her. *How did it happen to me?* He thought dazed and unhappy.

Mary was disappointed and upset. She looked at Paul's slippers and watch on the table next to the couch and began to cry.

As always, I screw up my relationship, She thought sadly.

She loved Paul and didn't know how to approach the matter wisely and delicately.

Of course, it was not just sex!

But wasn't it true? When did they talk without attacking each other and having sex?

Mary didn't like that feeling of loss, much less that she was crying.

She decided that she would treat Paul with indifference and that she would try to date someone. They say one love heals another.

She got up from the couch and went to take a shower. Tomorrow would be another day and she didn't want Paul in her life anymore. She'd give Robson, her colleague, a chance, and maybe she'd forget Paul. Robson had always loved her and made that very clear.

Paul decided to move on with his life and was getting busier and busier. His thoughts only intensified at night when he got home. He missed her and loved her more than anything, but he wouldn't look for her and he was determined to forget her.

It's been seven months since their last date when they loved each other so intensely. Paul craved her and thought of her every day. But he was determined and resolute and didn't want her in his life. She, in turn, also did not seek him out and was working more than ever, taking one shift after another so as not to have to run into him or think about him.

But when she was at home or even in the hospital, when she had a minute to think, she dreamed of his kisses and affectionate hugs.

The phone rang and Paul answered.

"Hello!"

"Paul, this is Wagner," said his friend on the other side of the line.

"Hey, buddy, how is it going? — Long time no see."

"You're the one who disappeared, man, is everything okay?"

"Yes, everything is fine, you?"

"We're fine, we're fine. I'm calling you to invite you to my engagement party," Wagner said very excited and full of joy.

"Man! That's awesome! Congratulations!" Paul was extremely happy for his friend and "compadre."

"Debby really got me," he said laughing loudly.

"I can see that. And when will it be?"

"Two months from now, but I'm already calling you in advance so you can get ready since we're having it in Hawaii."

"You're really cocky, huh?" He played with his friend.

"Yeah. We're chartering a plane for up to a hundred people and we're going to spend a whole weekend in Hawaii"

"You can count me there. I'm going to organize my schedule so that I'll be free."

"And Paul... you can bring a date, okay?"

"Thank you, buddy. There's just no one I want to take. I appreciate it anyway."

"OK. I'll give you the details later. Take care."

Wagner hung up and Paul stood still for a minute. His friend's happiness was evident and he was happy for it. Wagner deserved to be happy again, thought Paul.

He parked his car and went up to his office. He had a lot to do before the first hearing that day.

Mary rushed into the bookstore for she had wanted a book with decorating tips. Since she'd bought her apartment a year and three months ago, she hadn't decorated it the way she wanted. There was something missing there. She couldn't tell what, but with the help of several magazines, she'd find out.

She focused on looking at the pictures of several books and magazines. She put a pile before her to decide which one to take.

"This decorating book is excellent." Said a young man facing her on the large bench full of books.

"Sorry?" She looked frightened at the handsome, smiling man.

"I'm sorry I snooped around," he said giving the sexiest smile in the world.

"No, it's ok. I'm glad you snooped," she said with a smile.

"I don't know anything about decorating, so I came here to buy something that can guide me." She smiled charmingly.

"My name is Jason, very pleased to meet you, miss?" He asked by raising an eyebrow.

"Pleased to meet you. I'm Mary." She laughed at herself. "Nice to meet you."

"What do you want to decorate? I'm an architect and a decorator."

"I can't believe it! Really? I do hope you can help, Jason."

"Of course, Mary. Let's see what you've got so far." He moved around the bench and stood beside her.

As he rummaged through her pile of books, she squinted her eyes at him. He was blond with light brown eyes, a tapered nose, fleshy mouth, athletic body, tall, about thirty-four years old, and very well dressed.

"Did I get the right books and magazines?" She asked politely.

"How about we sit over there in the café with all these books and I'll help you choose?" He suggested.

"Let's go, then."

The two headed to the café inside the bookstore and the waiter came immediately. She ordered a cappuccino and Jason a mocha coffee.

As soon as the attendant left he looked her in the eye and said:

"What kind of environment do you want to decorate, Mary?"

"My apartment. It's got some things scattered around here and there, but I feel like something's missing. I've been living there for a little over a year, and I feel I have been too busy to dedicate myself to its decoration."

"Ok! Very busy then." He said staring at her.

"Yes." She answered without going into detail.

"If you want, we can schedule a day you're available so I can take a look and suggest something. How about that?" He said, already extending his card to her.

"Wow! I think that's great. How about this Friday? Would you have time?"

"Just a moment, let me check my schedule right here." He took his phone and moved his finger back and forth.

"I can be there at 7:00 p.m. if it's not too late for you." He said looking into her eyes.

"All right, 7:00 p.m. then, let's finish our coffee and I'll give you my address, okay?"

"OK. No problem." He said while sipping his coffee and looking at her.

Beautiful! He thought delighted.

The two talked for another half hour and Mary left in a hurry, saying she was late. They kissed each other on the cheek as she left.

Jason finished his coffee and was looking forward to next Friday to see Mary again and get to know her better. He had been delighted with her and knew that she liked him too.

Who knows, right? It's so hard to find someone for something serious, he smiled thoughtfully.

Already settled in her office and attending one patient after another, Mary no longer remembered the pleasant encounter with Jason.

"Dr. Taylor, your 6:00 o'clock patient apologized. He is going to be 20 minutes late. He said he's in a terrible traffic jam." Said her secretary.

"OK. Darah. Thank you! I'm going to rest a little then."

Mary took her computer and decided to search her new friend's name, to find out who he really was.

She was surprised to see his photo at various events in the city, receiving plaques and various awards as one of the best architects and decorators. They even mentioned his fortune.

Wow! She thought, gaping. He is so humble and nice. No one could tell he was so rich, she thought. He was wearing beautiful, very good quality clothes. She saw his pictures with several slim, beautiful women and realized that maybe he was more of a lady's man. Just below, she saw a note with a picture of him with a stunning blonde.

"Giselle and Jason, after two long years, end the engagement." The date was two years ago.

Mary was thoughtful and sorry for him. *They made a beautiful couple*, she thought.

She attended her last patient, who apologized a thousand times for the half-hour delay, which she didn't even see pass, and went home. She urgently needed a shower and something to eat.

Chapter Ten

Finally, the long-awaited Friday had arrived and Jason put together all his models, books, magazines, and albums to make a great presentation for Mary.

He'd really liked her and he was going to help her in any way he could. It'd been a long time since he'd been attracted to a woman like he was to her.

Mary was beautiful, charming, polite, sexy, and had a breathtaking ass.

"Can you send him up, please," replied Mary.

She had come home, showered and put on fresh clothes. The white t-shirt was made of silk and she was super comfortable. She was also barefoot.

She opened the door to wait for Jason and was looking forward to her new friend's visit.

"Hi!" She greeted him cheerfully.

"Hi!" he replied cheerfully, kissing Mary on the cheek.

"Come in. Make yourself at home."

He was also wearing shorts and a T-shirt and took off his

shoes as he entered her house.

"Beautiful, Mary!" he said, already looking with experienced and professional eyes.

"Come see the rest." She suggested excitedly.

"You have very good taste, I loved the pieces, but it's just lacking something else." He said looking into her eyes.

"I said so, didn't I?" she said, smiling and grabbing a bottle of wine and two glasses. "Let's have a drink while I go through the material you brought," she said, moving to the balcony and serving them wine.

"Delicious!" He said smiling and drinking again.

"What do you suggest?" She asked, laughing and drinking her wine too.

The two talked for three hours about various subjects and didn't even notice the time pass. Those were fun and magical moments and Mary was super happy to have met him.

He was charming, handsome, sexy, and very polite—a real gentleman.

He looked discreetly at Mary's ass, but she knew that all straight men really looked. *I don't believe it,* she thought smiling as she talked to him.

The two said goodbye and Jason was in charge of picking her up from the hospital on Monday for shopping. Mary was excited and cheerful like she hadn't been in a long time.

She loved Jason's ideas and noticed that he had good taste and an excellent eye to arrange furniture and objects in the environment like no one else.

She was very excited to decorate her house and leave her touch on everything.

Mary spent the whole weekend on duty and on Sunday night went to visit her mother.

"Mom." She said kissing her mother.

"I haven't seen you in ages. You look thinner." said her mother looking at her.

"I'm fine, Mom, don't worry. Fat doesn't mean healthy," she said with a smile.

"Come have some soup with me and catch up."

"Sure. I'm hungry," she said with a smile.

She stayed with her mother until midnight and came home to rest.

On Monday, she worked all morning and since there were no surgeries, she had lunch and went shopping around town with Jason.

He was nice and friendly all the time, and late in the afternoon, Mary invited him to go to her apartment. She'd whip up a homemade pizza for them. He thought that was a great idea.

"Oops!" He said after Mary dropped wine on his t-shirt.

"I'm so clumsy!" She said happily.

Jason took off his shirt and put it aside so it would dry out before he left. He had a strong and athletic body.

"You're beautiful, darling!" He said staring at Mary with lustful eyes, full of desire.

"Thanks! You're quite a man too." They both laughed and

Mary felt joyful and fulfilled.

Suddenly, the bell rang.

"Are you expecting someone?" He asked looking at Mary.

"No. Excuse me, I'll see who it is."

She opened the door and it was Paul.

"Hi!" She said smiling at him.

"How is everything?" He asked seriously.

"Everything's great."

"Mary, can I get the cheese from the fridge?" Jason said, appearing totally at ease near the door.

"Sure," she answered him.

"Good evening!" said Paul not looking too friendly.

"Good evening!" Jason answered politely.

"I'll be right there, darling. Go ahead and get the cheese, please," Mary said looking at him.

She looked at Paul as if she said "so"?

"I came to get my watch and slippers." He said in an icy voice.

"Just a moment, I'm going to get them. Do you want to come in?" She asked politely.

"No!" was his short and sweet answer.

"I'll get them," she said sweetly. Paul wanted to die.

Mary went to the balcony and picked up Paul's belongings from a chair.

"I see you've wasted no time." He said, taking his things from her hand and turning away.

Mary didn't say a word and closed the door. She didn't even wait for him to get in the elevator.

She went back to meet Jason on the balcony and drinking wine with Jason was no longer that fun, but she didn't let it show at all. The conversation between them went on normally and at the end of the evening, when she saw him to the door, he bent over and gave a kiss on her lips.

She kissed him back and felt absolutely nothing.

The two said goodbye and agreed to have lunch another day—a quick lunch near the hospital.

Mary sat on her couch in the living room and leaned her head, thinking of Paul. He was more beautiful than ever and thinner too. She felt sorry and missed him.

Paul was really angry.

Why the hell did he go to that insensitive woman's house? He wondered every second. *How stupid of me,*

She didn't waste any time. She was already with someone else there. She had a lot of nerve.

He was jealous, envious, and missing her, that was the truth, but Paul would never admit it.

The next day, Paul arrived at his firm quickly and went into his office. He had a client in ten minutes, and he wanted to be calmer.

"Mr. O'Brian, the client has arrived." Said his secretary opening the door and speaking in a low voice.

"Please, send her in. Thank you!" Paul got up from behind his desk.

An elegantly dressed lady came in and right after her a beautiful and very sexy girl.

"Good morning!" He greeted, reaching out to the lady's hand and then to the young woman.

"Good morning!" They replied each one shaking his hand.

"Please sit down." He said politely, indicating two super comfortable armchairs.

The two sat down and looked at him.

"So, what can I do for you?"

"My name is Sally, and this is my daughter Nicolle." Paul nodded.

"I've recently found out that my husband has had another wife for 24 years and I want to file a divorce."

"Right!" Paul said while taking notes on the paper in front of him. "Matrimonial assets?" He was asking and writing everything down quickly in totally illegible handwriting.

After an hour and a half of conversation and debate with the daughter inciting her mother all the time, Paul asked his secretary to bring them some coffee.

"So, please, bring me all the documents on the list. My secretary will prepare a power of attorney so that I can represent you in court and as soon as the complaint is ready, I will call you again, okay?" He said looking at Sally.

"All right, Mr. O'Brian. Thank you for your time."

"Could I have your card with your cell phone number, please?" asked Nicolle.

"Sure! Here it is."

Nicolle took the card, looked and gestured it to him.

"I can't see your personal phone number, just the office

phone."

She said pouting, nothing sexy.

"Oh! yes," he took the card back and wrote down his number. "Sorry!" He said softly.

She smiled and looked at that Greek god.

Paul saw five more clients, all of them wanting a divorce. He came home exhausted due to numerous discussions. When the couple went together, there was not always a consensus and it all ended in fights and serious arguments. It was a real sordid affair.

He barely got home when his cell phone rang. He looked at the number and he didn't recognize it. He decided to take it.

"Hello!" he said taking off the tie.

"Paul?" he heard a voice from an unknown woman.

"Yes, it's me. Who is it?" he asked curiously.

"It's me, Nicolle. I was in your office today with my mother, remember?"

"Hello, of course, I remember. Is she okay? Do you need anything?" he asked worriedly.

"We're fine, Paul. Listen, do you want to go out for a drink?" she asked suddenly.

"Sure. How about tomorrow?" he said excitedly.

"Today. Can you?" she said in a voice that wouldn't take no for an answer.

She's not shy at all, Paul thought.

"Nicolle, I'm sorry. I just got home and I'm exhausted." He said on his way to his room.

"How about I come to your place? I promise not to talk about my parents' divorce," she said anxiously.

Paul was very tired, but if she was willing to do that, that's fine by him. "Why not?"

"OK. Let me give you the address," he said more excited.

In less than an hour, his intercom rang announcing Nicolle.

"Come in, welcome," he said, giving her a kiss on her cheek.

"Oh goodness, Paul! Your penthouse is beautiful." She said admiring the pleasant atmosphere.

"Thank you."

Nicolle was nowhere near poor, her parents had a very good estate and she was an only child.

She stopped in front of him, and she was very sexy in tiny shorts and a tank top. She wasn't wearing a bra and had very little make-up on. Her perfume was soft and as she was beautiful.

"Would you like a glass of wine?" he asked on his way to his cellar.

"Yes, please." She spoke looking at Paul provocatively.

They had wine and talked luxuries.

The conversation was boring and Paul was almost asleep.

Nicolle noticed that and came closer to him in the rocking chair. Without delay, she spread her legs and straddled his lap.

"Oops!" He smiled, grabbing her by the waist.

"I've been wanting you since the moment I saw you, beautiful lawyer." She spoke already kissing Paul.

He kissed her back, but that couldn't be described as a

sensual kiss. They had sex twice and she left satisfied, but she was leaving behind a tired and depressed Paul.

He felt appalled that while he was having sex with that beautiful woman, all he could think about was Mary and the fire the two of them felt when they were together. He hated himself for that and promised to forget Mary's existence.

The days went by fast and turned into months and came the big day of Wagner's engagement.

Everyone was supposed to be at the airport at exactly 9:00 a.m. Paul talked to Wagner to see if all the hundred seats were taken and Paul asked Wagner if he could take Nicolle. He didn't want to go to the engagement party alone and the two were gradually getting along.

Chapter Eleven

"Good morning!" Paul said to a nervous and restless Wagner.

"Good morning, brother!" Said Wagner giving Paul a hug and admiring the beautiful blonde next to Paul.

"That's Nicolle," Paul said, smiling with his eyes.

"Very pleased to meet you, Nicolle. How did you get this guy?"

Wagner was very happy and overjoyed.

"I haven't hooked him yet." She replied smiling and she really was a beautiful woman.

"Make yourselves comfortable. We're going to wait for more people to get here so we can all get on the plane together." Wagner said at the same time as he ran to receive another guest.

The guests were arriving in pairs. Paul thanked God for taking Nicolle. *I don't want to be the third wheel for many couples*, he thought.

He'd never cared about being single and wanted to stay

that way, but it was boring to go to another state in a place as beautiful as Hawaii and not have company.

And Nicolle wasn't all bad; she just didn't have a very developed mind. She droned on and sometimes Paul just wanted to keep quiet and she didn't understand that. *Things of youth!* He thought bored.

She was beautiful and young, twenty-four years old and knew how to be pushy, thought Paul looking at her, fiddling with her cell phone.

It was only when Paul raised his head that he saw it. Mary and another young man coming towards the plane.

What the hell was she doing there? Who had invited her? He thought.

He was already possessed by jealousy.

Mary hadn't seen him yet and Paul decided to "hide" behind a fat guy who was also waiting outside.

Mary was gorgeous!

In light blue shorts and a white tank top, which made her beautiful and hard breasts even more beautiful. The shorts were short and showed off her beautiful legs and lush curves. She was relaxed, smiling, and had all the attention from the young man on her side.

Could it be the same guy I saw in the apartment? Paul asked himself as he looked at them, trying not to draw attention.

He loved and desired her so much. Lord, give me strength, he thought. He wished he'd forgotten her, but he didn't.

"Glad you guys could make it!" He heard Wagner greet the young man with an affectionate hug and then kiss Mary on the cheek.

When did they get so close? Paul wondered, angry that Wagner had not told him that his doctor would be on the same flight.

Mary ran her eyes over everyone and didn't see Paul, who was still behind the fat man.

They were all invited to get on the plane and formed a long line. Mary and the boy had already positioned themselves and Paul praised God for being much farther behind her.

He could see that there was an intimacy between them and that Mary was happy.

He grew jealous and upset.

The line was moving slowly and everyone settled on the plane. They sat on the first seat that was empty so Mary wouldn't see them.

"Is everything all right?" Asked Nicolle looking at him.

"Yes. I don't understand the question," he answered defensively.

"You suddenly got weird. You seem that you don't want to be noticed." She said looking at him.

"Where did that come from, baby?" Paul laughed awkwardly and kept fiddling with his cell phone.

He started hating that trip and more so for bringing

Nicolle with him.

The flight lasted three hours and forty-five minutes. Hawaii's airport was full of tourists arriving or returning home.

Paul took a breath as soon as the flight attendant announced that everyone could disembark.

"Let's wait until everyone has moved along. There's no hurry." He said holding Nicolle's arm.

"OK, as you please," she replied with a smile.

Paul concluded that it was easy to deal with her because everything he said or suggested she would agree as if she never had a formed opinion about anything.

Everyone came down smiling and excited when he saw from afar that Mary was coming all cheerful with the blond young man, he turned his face and stared out the window.

"Shall we?" Nicolle called after everyone had already disembarked.

"Yes, let's go." Paul took his and Nicolle's luggage from the overhead compartment and the two came down. She led the way.

Five buses from the hotel were waiting to take them to the resort. Paul noticed that Mary and her date were on the second bus. He once again sighed relieved.

Of course, they would meet, but first, he wanted to let the shock of the first moment pass.

Mary was happy to have accepted Jason's invitation to his sister Debby's wedding.

She hadn't had the opportunity to travel to Hawaii yet and

she was finding everything beautiful, very colorful, and fun.

"Have you ever been here, Jason?" Asked Mary approaching him on the bus.

"Yes. Dad used to bring us here every summer. The holidays were magical. I think that's why they decided to come here." He said smoothly.

Jason proved to be a great companion, friend, and host. They had already had sex, but it there was no fire. Mary compared him with Paul all the time; there was no way it could be any different. She was still in love with him.

She hadn't seen him anymore and that was good. She could forget that one day they made love.

"Is everything all right? You were suddenly distant," Jason said looking at Mary's face.

"Yes. I was thinking about my Mom. One day, I'm going to bring her here."

Lied Mary with a poker face and smiling.

"We can arrange something like this. What do you think?" He asked excitedly.

"We'll see..."

Mary didn't want to give him false hope. She enjoyed his company, he was pleasant, kind, polite, loving, and handsome, but there was no chemistry between them.

She thought of Paul again in a daze. That blue-eyed Greek god. He was all she wanted most, but unfortunately, they didn't match. They fought all the time.

Making love to Paul was crazy and she got turned on just

to think about it. He made her feel beautiful, hot, sexy, and like a much-loved woman. The last time they were together, he kissed her like never before after they had sex. He was so affectionate! She began to get sad and Jason noticed it.

"Tired, darling?" he asked willingly.

"A little, I worked a lot last night and I didn't sleep very well last night." It was the most plausible answer she found.

She felt she had to beware of her thoughts, for she was being watched by Jason all the time. He noticed everything.

"You will have a whole weekend to rest and take it easy, so let's have fun, get in this wonderful sea, sunbathe.

"It will be wonderful, I'm sure of it." She said with a smile.

"Thank you, Jason! For inviting me."

"I thank you for coming, dear." Jason approached and kissed her on her lips.

Everyone who arrived was staying in the corner of the great lobby so that they were welcomed by Debby and Wagner, who arrived before they did. After everyone was present, Wagner said:

"Welcome, all of you. Enjoy the beach, the hotel pool, and later on in the evening, our engagement party." Everyone clapped their hands and let out cheers.

"In your rooms, you will find a costume and a brochure with instructions. Read it carefully." Wagner smiled with satisfaction.

Mary and Jason were going to be in the room on the first floor. They took the keycards with the number five on it. They both went to the bedroom to settle in.

Paul and Nicolle's room was number six, right next door to Mary and Jason."

Only they didn't know that.

Paul didn't see Mary around and he was happy about it.

"Look, Paul, how cool!" Cried Nicolle to him.

"What is this?" He asked him as he picked up a costume and a mask.

"How creative! It's going to be a masquerade ball and we'll be in costumes. That's so cool!"

"So that's why all the guests had to take that questionnaire, asking for the size of clothes, slipper and shoes, and all that stuff." He smiled having fun.

"Do you think each couple is going to wear a different costume?" Asked Nicolle.

"I don't know, but this room was already reserved for us. It's probably going to be a different costume for each couple, right? Otherwise, what's the fun in that?" He smiled picking up his costume.

"Which one is yours, Paul?"

"Superman."

"Wow! You're going to look really sexy in those tights." She said coming on to him.

He swerved and went to the window. He didn't feel like having sex then. He was tired and seeing Mary bothered him.

"We will all go looking the same, Nicolle." Look at the brochure with all the explanations.

"It is going to be a kind of game, where each couple will be in the same costume and will mingle in the hall. We're going to have to go dancing until we find our date." He went on reading and explaining everything to Nicolle.

"That explains the wig. Where's the fun if you saw my blond hair and recognized me?" She said.

"What about the women's costumes? What is it?" Paul was curious.

"Wonder Woman," she smiled like a child.

It will be very interesting to see all the women wearing Wonder Woman costumes and all the men like Superman." They smiled amused. "I bet this was all Debby's idea. She's very fun, smart, and cheerful." He chuckled.

"What do you want to do first?" He asked.

"Shall we go to the beach? We can have a meal there and come back later to get ready for the engagement ball. What do you think?"

"That's a great idea. Let's go to a more distant beach. Here it will be very crowded." He said excitedly.

"I'm going to change then," She said, already opening her suitcase and picking up her beautiful bikini, hat, pareo, and a beautiful beach bag.

Paul and Nicolle took the boat the hotel offered and went to a distant beach and spent the day. They came back exhausted at 4:00 p.m. to rest and get ready for the big engagement ball.

Mary and Jason enjoyed the beach in the morning, facing

the hotel and in the afternoon went to an antique fair.

At 5:00 p.m., they returned to the hotel to rest.

The hours flew by and when they noticed, it was time for the dance. Both Paul and Nicolle were perfect and unrecognizable. They both laughed at their costumes and were cheerful and amused.

As they opened the bedroom door to leave, they ran into Mary and Jason in costume. Paul recognized her at once and knew it was her, but she didn't know he was Paul.

Everyone greeted one another smiling and Paul noticed Mary's ass. *Beautiful and sexy!*

They went to the ballroom together and separated there. When they were all gathered, the DJ announced that everyone should start to mix among themselves, so that when the music started, they should dance until they find their pair. And so did the hundred guests.

Paul knew where Mary was, just by the ass, and went after her. Some couples were already dancing and he ran to Mary and took her in his arms. She laughed at herself having fun, not knowing she was in Paul's arms.

"You're not my date," she said smiling happily.

Paul kept turning with Mary in his arms without saying a word and gave no chance of her dodging him.

A slow song began and the couples were getting apart and picking up other pairs, but Paul held Mary by the waist, leading her to the middle of the hall.

The attraction between them was incredible and she said:

"You remind me of someone I knew." She said softly and leaned over him.

"And is this a dream or a nightmare?"

"It would be a dream." She said not recognizing his voice.

He squeezed her more in his arms and hugged her with both hands around her waist.

"Please, you're squeezing me too much." Protested Mary walking away.

She loved that approach, but she wouldn't let him notice that. The stranger had the same athletic built as Paul.

Paul loosened the hug and Mary breathed a sigh of relief.

"We need to switch pairs." Said Mary looking aside and not seeing anyone coming within reach, so she kept dancing.

She decided to lay her head on the man's shoulder and relax, enjoying the music. Paul smelled her hair and closed his eyes, dreaming of Mary in his arms. Not being able to resist any longer, Paul put his hands on her back and pressed her against him. Mary stiffened and said:

"Paul? Is that you?" her voice was sweet and showed surprise.

Not saying a word, the stranger hugged her tighter and was touching Mary's hair with his lips. She looked at him and not resisting any longer, he took Mary's face with both hands and kissed her.

Mary immediately recognized her great love and returned the wet, long, sexy and delicious kiss.

Paul kissed Mary as if he needed to suck all her soul and

Mary corresponded stunned.

He'd move his hands on her back and brought her against his chest. Paul moved his mouth close to her ear and spoke in a hoarse and passionate voice.

"You make me crazy, my love. I need you. Let's meet outside?" he suggested softly.

Mary gave a no and Paul went on.

"I'm going to walk out that side door and meet you behind that rock with the coconut trees, okay? We have to do this now since they haven't joined the pairs yet."

Paul let Mary go and she almost fell, so wobbly that she was. She looked everywhere and did not recognize Jason in any of them and decided to go out after Paul.

"Mary?" called Paul softly.

"What does that mean, Paul?" She asked angrily with her hands on her hips. "Are you following me?" She looked at him with an annoyed face.

"Mary, come here," Paul said taking Mary by the hand and moving away into the darkness of the beach.

When they got close to the sea, it was so dark and they saw the hotel at a good distance.

"I'm not following you, Mary. I came to my best friend and compadre's wedding," He said, taking off his mask and putting it in his pocket.

Mary also removed her mask and looked at him.

They both laughed as they looked at their costumes and Mary was no longer so angry.

"Right," she said with a smile.

"How did you get here? Do you know Debby?"

"Yes. I came with her brother Jason." She said sweetly.

Paul was very jealous of Mary.

"Are you two dating?" He asked anxiously.

"Kind of," she replied, "we're getting to know each other to see what happens."

"Mary..." before she could say something, Paul threw himself at her, kissing her mouth urgently and greedily. Mary lost balance and they both fell to the ground. Paul lay on Mary without stopping to kiss her and said, panting:

"Mary... Mary... Mary..."

"Let me go Paul, you're crazy, stop it, let me go now!" She said, angry.

Paul let her go. She got up and ran back to the ballroom. She was panting and with the wig all crooked. She went into the bathroom to get it together.

How did she let that happen? She thought devastated. She fixed her wig, touched up her makeup, cleaned her clothes that were full of sand, put on her mask, and went back to the ballroom.

She found Jason and took his hand smiling.

"Where were you, darling?" He asked. "Come on, let's sit down for dinner."

"Did they all find their pairs?" She asked smilingly.

"I think so. Debby's idea was very fun and creative."

Mary saw it when Paul came into the room and went to

the restroom. He also needed to groom up.

Everyone took off their masks to eat and enjoy the party to the fullest. After dinner, they were going to play bingo and there would be lots of prizes for the guests.

This ball would be marked in the history of Hawaii.

The food was delicious and there were still two seats left at their table.

"Who's going to sit here, Jason? I can't read the names," Mary asked as she turned her head.

They're a couple of friends of Debby and Wagner's.

"Good evening!" Paul spoke hand in hand with Nicolle.

"Good evening!" The other four couples at the table answered. Mary looked at Paul, who was stiff as a board. She thought apprehensively, "this is not going to work."

She was very jealous of Paul seeing him holding hands with that beautiful, exuberant blonde.

He didn't look at her once and dinner went on in the most perfect order.

"My friends!" Wagner and Debby appeared, holding hands and smiling at their table.

"Have you seen Dr. Taylor, Paul? " asked Wagner loud and clear.

"I hadn't seen her." Paul looked at her and said, "How are you, Dr. Taylor?" He asked sarcastically.

"I'm fine. Thanks!" She answered politely.

Chapter Twelve

Mary and Jason ate in silence and then decided to take a walk on the beach before bingo began.

Paul didn't feel like playing bingo, but Nicolle was so excited and cheerful that he decided to do what she wanted.

The game turned out to be super fun and everyone stayed up late playing.

The prizes were beautiful and sophisticated.

Wagner tastes were definitely of a millionaire and everyone was loving the party.

The next day, everyone could enjoy the beach, since they would catch the plane at 2 p.m.

Paul got up early, though he went to bed too late. He wanted to enjoy the beach, but Nicolle wanted to sleep. He left her asleep and went to the beach alone. The day was beautiful and the sun was weak.

Paul sat on a bench away from the hotel facing the sea.

He gazed at the blue-green sea and closed his eyes. He received the breeze and mentally thanked God for all that.

"Good morning! Am I disturbing you?" Asked Mary, gently approaching the bench and waiting for an answer to sit down.

Paul opened his eyes and looked at the love of his life.

"No. Not at all, please, sit down." He said quietly and politely.

Mary sat next to Paul, and his leg touched hers and they both felt a shiver to the bones.

"Paul..."

"Mary..."

They spoke at the same time and laughed at each other.

"You first," he said.

"Paul, I'd like to talk to you when we get back. Do you agree?" She asked sweetly and gave him a charming smile.

"I would love that," he replied looking at her. "Mary? I would like to apologize for yesterday." He said looking into her eyes.

"We'll talk about it later. What happened happened, and I was guilty too," she spoke sweetly.

He just looked at her and wished to be in her arms.

"So it's settled then: I'll get in touch when we get back because I don't know if I'm going to have surgery on Monday and what time I'm going to be home." She said.

"OK. I'll be waiting for your call," he said staring into Mary's green eyes.

She looks even more beautiful in this color. He thought he felt like hugging and kissing her.

"I see you've got a tan?" He said looking at the tan lines and at Mary's bare legs.

"Yes. I didn't even ask for that!" She said excitedly. "Can you imagine if I stayed here for a week? Sure, I'd come home much more tanned." She laughed at herself and looked into Paul's eyes.

"You'd look gorgeous!" That was his answer.

"Is it serious with her? That child you're dating?" She asked looking into his eyes.

"You know it isn't. I just didn't want to be in such a beautiful place and completely alone, thinking of you." He said calmly.

Mary just shook her head and put her hand on the bench near Paul. She looked at that immense sea and closed her eyes, feeling the warm breeze.

"I love you, Mary!" Paul said taking her hand.

Mary opened her eyes and closed them again, avoiding to kiss Paul. Her emotions were penetrating deep.

"Oh! Paul! I love you too, and I want everything to work out between us." She said looking at him and turning her gaze to his blue eyes.

"That's my goal, Mary." He said holding her hand with affection and emotion.

"That's why we need to talk." She said holding his hand firmly.

She got up and kissed him on the cheek and left in a hurry. He loves me! Her joy could be seen from a mile away.

He loves me! She kept repeating mentally to herself and

smiling so silly.

She would be ready for this conversation and make a decision in her life.

She would follow Sissy's advice and love Paul with all her strength. She wouldn't be afraid to love and let herself be loved, she thought happily.

Paul was over the moon with joy, knowing that Mary loved him too.

Oh, thank you, God! He looked at the sea and thanked God with a smile.

Everyone had a delightful lunch and at 2 p.m. the buses arrived to take the guests to the airport.

Mary was happy and certain that everything would work out in her life.

She'd finish whatever it was with Jason and thank him for the happy, lukewarm days they had together, she thought smiling.

Everyone got to their seats on the plane smiling and talking about the beautiful party. Mary looked at everyone.

Jason was a lovely person, but Mary did not love him as a man but as a friend and felt that Jason also considered her to be a friend, she thought looking at him by her side, already asleep. Paul was seated five rows behind Mary and Nicolle wouldn't stop talking. At any moment, she would have something to talk about or show on her cell phone.

She was a good girl, but Paul would put an end to all this. He was tired of Nicolle. She was beautiful and deserved someone her age and who loved her.

"You're thoughtful today, Paul," Nicolle said holding his hand.

"We need to talk to Nicolle," Paul said, turning himself to face her.

Nicolle looked at him and already knew they were going to break up.

"All right, Paul, I know what you're going to say." She said, letting go of his hand and filling her eyes with water.

"You're beautiful and very interesting, but I don't love you as I should."

He spoke fondly and very softly for only her to hear.

"I have a great affection for you and nothing more. I'd rather tell you that now than keep doing what we are doing."

"You're a beautiful and honest man. Thank you for this wonderful trip. I loved it." She said sadly.

"I also enjoyed being with you, but we can be friends. We don't need to cut ties."

"No, Paul! I don't want to see you with anyone else. I'd rather keep you in my past." She was firm and absolute.

Paul didn't say a word and closed his eyes to think of Mary. She loved him too. He was very happy about it.

The flight went on and everyone was happy.

They said goodbye joyfully and Paul took a look at Mary discreetly and loved her even more.

"I'll drop you at your house, Nicolle," Paul said, taking their luggage.

"All right," she said, dry.

Nicolle and Paul were silent all the way. Paul had no

desire to talk to Nicolle.

She was too immature, he thought unhappily.

"Thank you, Paul." Said Nicolle getting out of the car and picking up her luggage and turning her back without even looking at him.

Oh well, thought Paul. Life goes on.

Paul turned around the corner and took the road to his apartment. He was too happy to let Nicolle deter him with her tantrums.

He decided to play his favorite songs from his phone. He turned his attention to the dashboard and didn't see a big runaway truck coming towards him. Before he could swerve, the truck crashed badly into Paul's car. It was a matter of seconds.

The car flipped twice, so intense was the hit and the airbag opened in the face of a totally unconscious Paul.

A woman who was behind Paul's car saw the accident and pulled over on the side of the road.

She came out of her car in horror at the crash and imagined that whoever was in that car would certainly be dead. The car was wrecked. She ran to the car while she called 911. She wasn't sure of anything as she replied to the phone operator who said he would send an ambulance as soon as possible.

She stayed there waiting for help to arrive and took all of Paul's belongings. She'd go to the hospital after the ambulance and get in touch with the family.

The young man was handsome and young, he would

surely make it out of this one, she thought praying.

Daisy had already lost a son like that and she didn't want that suffering for any mother. She prayed for the young man the whole time.

Upon admission to the hospital, they recognized him as a patient there and warned Daisy. She called his relatives and waited for them so she could give them his belongings.

By the time Mary got home, they'd already called her to the hospital. It was urgent and they needed her—car accident with major fractures and trauma.

Mary left in a hurry and in five minutes, she got to the hospital and went straight to the operating room.

"Man or woman," asked Mary to one of her surgical assistants.

"Man," answered the man.

"Let's go!" She said, already coming in and asking her assistants for information. There were two other surgeons in the room who brought her up to date. The case was very serious.

"We're losing the patient." An assistant yelled when she looked at the heart monitor attached to Paul.

"What's his name?" Mary asked as she was about to start the resuscitation.

"Paul," answered the girl.

Mary refused to believe she meant her Paul. The love of her life.

"Come on, Paul, please!" Mary spoke desperately while doing the massage on his heart. After half an hour of trying to revive Paul, Mary said:

"Please, take over, Peter," asked Mary exhausted.

Peter was a tall, strong doctor and massaged Paul hard. Soon Paul breathed and the monitor line began to go back to normal.

"We need to do the surgery fast. He's losing a lot of blood. Send a request for more blood, Denise," said Mary, already opening Paul with a scalpel.

The bleeding had to be controlled there and now they could save him.

Mary prayed mentally and talked to Paul as well.

"You'll be fine, Paul," she said out loud and confident.

The surgery lasted nine hours and Mary was shaking from head to toe. She did everything she could to save the great love of her life and as she left the operating room, she sat in another room, took off her gloves, washed her hands and face, and began to cry.

"What is wrong, Dr. Taylor?" One of her assistants sat beside her and hugged her.

"I can't lose him, Denise," she said, crying.

"Everything is going to be all right, doctor. Let's wait the usual 48 hours and everything will be fine."

"Thank you, Denise," said Mary tired and frustrated.

"Can you talk to his family? I'm going to take a shower. I'm going to spend the night here at the hospital. I want to follow him closely," She said as she got up and thanked Denise.

Mary took a shower and put on her hospital clothes. She

got a chair and sat next to Paul in the ICU.

He was now stable and asleep. He was in an induced coma because he had hit his head badly in the rollover of the car and there was a worrying clot.

"My darling, get better. I love you!" she said softly holding his hand.

At dawn, the monitor whistled loudly and Mary saw that Paul was suffering cardiac arrest again.

Everyone in the ICU came running and together, they tried to resuscitate and used the defibrillator on Paul.

Unfortunately, Paul had to be intubated. He would go on sedated. Mary didn't go back to sleep and watched Paul the rest of the night.

She talked to him and told him all about her life, sometimes laughing at her stories, sometimes crying.

"I love you, my darling! Get well soon, we'll be together, don't leave me alone. You are the love of my life." Mary said holding Paul's hand.

Chapter Thirteen

Knock. Knock. Knock.

"Come in," said Moses.

"Good morning," Mary appeared at the door, looking more downcast than anything.

"Are you all right, my dear?" asked Moses, frightened by Mary's appearance.

"I haven't slept well, but I'm fine." She replied, hugging him and kissing him on the cheek.

"Sit down, dear." He said looking at her and crossing his hands on the table.

"I need a few days off. Only three days." She said beginning to cry.

"Oh! Honey!" Moses went around the table and sat beside her on another chair, hugging her. "What happened?" He was careful and caring, as a father should be.

"Moses, I finally found the love of my life." She said sniffing.

"But that's wonderful! It is no reason to cry but to celebrate." He said smiling.

"He's in a bad state in the ICU. I operated on him yesterday." She started crying and sobbing again.

Moses hugged her and said:

"Take as long as you need and use all the resources and doctors available in this hospital. Shake heaven and earth and save this lucky guy."

Mary spoke as she got up, "thank you, my friend."

"You did everything within your reach, dear. God is in charge now. He will protect the man you love." Moses spoke with such conviction that Mary left the room much more hopeful that Paul would be fine.

"How is he?" Asked Paul's mother on the ICU visit.

"He's not well, Mrs. O'Brian, but let's have faith in God," Mary answered by comforting Aurora, who hugged her weeping.

"I can't afford to lose another son," she said sobbing.

"Please, calm down! He is surrounded by the best doctors. Everything will be fine. I'm going to spend the night here with him," she said smiling at Aurora.

"Thank you so much, Dr. Taylor, for doing this for my Paul."

"Please, call me Mary."

"OK. Thanks, Mary!" She said moved.

At dawn, Paul had a fever and became very agitated wanting to remove the breathing tube. Mary had him restrained and gave him an antipyretic along with something to calm him down.

After three days Paul had been in the hospital, Mary came down to talk to his parents and sister.

"Today, we will begin weaning Paul. That is, we will start removing the sedation slowly so that we can remove the tube. Let's see how he reacts to that."

Upon returning to Paul's bedside in the ICU, Mary spoke to him.

"It's going to be okay, darling. You're going to make it." Mary said fondly, always passing her hand over his hair, face, and arm. She wanted him to feel her presence.

"Today, I'm going to tell you how hard it was to do medicine. I had to face many hardships."

After three days they removed his tube.

Paul reacted well to the removal of the device and breathed without any assistance. That was a big win.

"How's your great love, my dear?" Moses entered the ICU box, asking and giving Mary a hug.

"Thank God he is reacting well, Moses. Thank you, darling." She stared at him with a tired look.

"Don't you think you'd better go home and get some rest? I'm going to ask someone to be with him all the time. Trust me!" Moses was calm, and she agreed to go home, take a shower, and get some sleep, with the promise that if there were any changes Mary would be called immediately.

"Honey, quiet your heart. He's going to be fine."

Mary hugged Moses for long minutes and felt immense peace. She could tell that Paul would really be fine.

Mary went home and barely entered her apartment when the intercom rang; it was Jason.

She took a deep breath and told the doorman to let him in.

"Hi, Jason!" greeted Mary holding the door.

"I was worried you wouldn't answer your phone." He said kissing Mary's forehead. It was when he noticed how downcast and tired she looked.

"Please, come in. Let's talk over here." She brought him to the balcony.

"Is everything all right, Mary?" He stared at her shocked by her appearance.

"Jason, we haven't had time to talk about this, and I think this is the best time." She said looking into his eyes.

"All right, honey, I know there's no love between us but a great friendship."

"Oh! Dear! I don't ever want to hurt you. That's never been my intention." She said dispiritedly.

"You're not hurting me. But there are things we feel before they're even said." He smiled faintly.

"I know," she said.

"Let's still be friends, right?" He joked winking at her.

"Yes. Friends forever!" She smiled.

"So I have to go. I have to meet a client who lives nearby. I came by just to see how things were going."

"Everything is fine. I wish you all the best in this life, Jason." She said sweetly.

"I wish you the same. Take care of yourself!"

"And Jason, thank you for this beautiful apartment. The décor is really wonderful."

"Yes. It's really nice, isn't it?"

They said goodbye with a hug and two kisses on the cheek.

Mary ran to the bathroom and took a warm and relaxing bath. She lay on his bed in her bathrobe and fell asleep instantly. She woke up at 4:00 in the morning.

She called the hospital and they informed her that Paul was fine and had no fever.

Mary breathed, relieved.

Mary returned to work normally in the surgeries and in her office and Paul was still asleep, giving no sign that he would wake up any time soon. Mary's concern was that he would have gaps in his memory.

He'd been in intensive care for two months already.

"I'm going to stay with him a little bit before my surgery. Go have a snack and come back in an hour, okay?" Mary told the nurse that was with Paul.

Mary took Paul's hand and began talking with him in a very low voice.

"My love, I'm starting to get very upset with you. Open those beautiful eyes and give me a beautiful smile. Come on? Have faith... you will make it! I will be right here." She whispered looking at him.

Suddenly, Mary turned to pick up a chair and heard behind her:

"Mary?" Paul said in a weak voice opening his eyes.

"My love! You heard me!" Mary cried and kissed him on her forehead.

"I'm feeling so weak and sick. What happened to me?"

he asked, turning slowly to Mary and looking sleepy at her.

"You were in a car accident and you were very hurt. But everything will be all right," she said, taking his hand.

"Is Mom downstairs?" He asked in a low voice.

"Yes. Do you want to see her? She's very worried about you, darling."

"I'd like to see her and tell her I'll be fine soon." He whispered, sleepy.

"I'll send for her."

Mrs. O'Brian took the elevator crying, thinking her son was dead. She was nervous and apprehensive.

She washed her hands, used the alcohol-based hand sanitizer, and put on the disposable smock to get into the ICU.

"What is it, Mary?" She rushed in, wiping her eyes with a paper towel.

"Don't cry, Mrs. O'Brian. He asked to see you. But he fell asleep again." Mary was very happy and hugged her.

"Oh! That's wonderful, Mary! I'm so happy." Paul's mother approached and took her son's hand.

"Oh, my son! How are you doing?" She lowered herself and kissed his forehead.

Paul opened his beautiful blue eyes and gave a faint smile.

"Mom!" He said with great difficulty and returning to sleep soundly.

Aurora cried, clinging to Mary and she reassured her that everything would be fine.

The days passed by quickly and Paul was recovering and

getting better every day.

After three and a half months in the ICU, he'd been moved to a regular room recently.

"You need be a little more patience, Paul," Mary spoke to him sweetly.

"Mary, I want to go home, you'll be there too and Mom has already made her employee available to take care of me. I'll be fine."

He went on trying to convince Mary that he would be better off at home.

"Really, it is easier to get an infection in a hospital. I'm going to go through everything and if all goes well, tomorrow I'll discharge you. Being discharged doesn't mean you can go around driving and going back to work."

"Can I work from home?" He asked smiling.

"When did you become so handsome?" asked Mary, smiling and giving a kiss on his lips.

"Thank you, Mary, for being you!" He was moved and hugged her.

"I love you dear, and I've never been so afraid in my life." She was pure sweetness.

"I love you too, Mary!" He pulled her so as to kiss her with love and tenderness. It was a passionate kiss, full of desire.

"You please behave!" She said, disengaging herself gently.

"It's okay, Mary. I'm feeling good." Paul was ruddy and in a good mood and very thin, but Mary decided that she would discharge him the next morning.

"All right, I'm going to work, and before I go home, I'm going to stop by and see you again."

Mary called Aurora and told her the news and asked to pick him up at 9:00 a.m. She had surgery and couldn't take him home.

"All right, my dear, you've done more than you should." Aurora would be very grateful to Mary for taking such good care of her son," she thought happily.

Paul went home and Mary slept with him in his large, spacious bed every day. He wasn't ready to make love yet, but Mary was looking forward to it, and so was Paul.

Fifteen days flew by and Paul was already working full steam at home and with his cell phone all the time.

Wagner and Debby's wedding was going to take place in two months, and he and Mary would be best man and bridesmaid respectively. He was happy for his friend.

"So Wagner, how are you feeling, anxious?" Asked Paul, pointing to his friend the armchair near him.

"I didn't remember getting married was so much trouble," Wagner said, smiling from ear to ear.

It was really nice to see his friend smiling again.

Debby is beautiful, man! Very talented and fun." Paul said smiling too.

"Yes. She's all that and more Paul. It's all working out super fine with the kids. Sometimes I forget she's home. Did you know she is better than Mark on video games? The four of them play and leave me out, and it's an endless shouting match at home." He was talking and shaking his head.

"I never thought I'd be happy again," Wagner said with his eyes watered. "She makes me want to struggle harder and harder."

"Are you fulfilling all the wishes of this beautiful woman?" Asked Paul smiling.

"We are even bringing a camel to our wedding! Tell me if that's not fulfilling her wish?" Wagner laughed with joy.

"Yes. Yes." Said Paul with a smile as well.

"What about you and Mary? How are things?" Asked the friend while taking his cold lemonade.

"We're fine. I'm going to ask her to marry me, Wagner." He said with a smile.

"Already? Are you sure about that?" Wagner was teasing Paul.

"She's the woman of my life."

"You can see that!" The two friends laughed together. They talked for another hour before Wagner went back to his office.

Chapter Fourteen

Mary was anxious with her evening plans to go home, take a shower and go to Paul's house.

They had many things in common and the conversation between them flowed so well that they didn't notice time pass by.

They really loved each other very much, thought Mary taking the elevator.

"OK. Debby, so I'll be waiting for you tomorrow here." Paul said very excitedly.

"I hope you know what you're doing, Paul," Debby said smiling happily for her friend.

"I'm sure of that Debby, see you tomorrow and thank you very much."

"You can always count on me, Paul," said Debby hanging up. Paul called his friend's jeweler and made an appointment to meet him the next afternoon.

Mary hadn't cleared Paul to drive yet, but he already felt good and would drive to the jeweler and then stop by the office.

Mary won't get to know anything, he thought happily.

"Oh, yes, darling. I'll be in surgery all afternoon," Mary told Paul.

"I thought we could have lunch together," he said hopefully.

"I'm sorry, my love, but today it will be impossible," she said regretfully. She knew he was feeling lonely, but their work required dedication and professionalism.

Paul arrived at the jeweler around 1:50 p.m. his friend was already waiting for him.

"How are you, Paul?" Andy came to meet him when he opened the door.

"I'm much better," he replied with a smile and already sitting on the nearest chair.

"Are you ok to drive?" he asked worried.

"I'm feeling great," Paul replied with a smile.

"So let's go downstairs. I have wonderful pieces I know will please you," he said, leading the way for an anxious and happy Paul behind him.

"I'm sure I'll find something beautiful for Mary."

"Sure! Now, let's see."

The engagement and wedding rings were all laid out on red cloth on a large table. There were about 15 rings.

Paul was delighted with all of them and there was a girl with beautiful hands and perfect nails to try them so that the client could get an idea of what the jewel would look like on the bride's finger.

Paul was dazzled by several rings and decided to buy

an engagement ring and a wedding ring. Both beautiful and very expensive.

But Paul was quite well off, so that wasn't a problem. He paid cash and kept the box in his jacket pocket.

He stopped by his office and everyone there came to hug him. He didn't see Debby anywhere and decided to put his anxiety aside and wait for his friend the next day at his house. He said goodbye to everyone, went back home and put on a comfortable outfit and began working hard on his cases. He hardly noticed the time passing and Mary coming into the house.

"Paul?" called Mary from the stairs.

"I'm here, honey, in my office," Paul answered, closing his computer and standing up to receive Mary with open arms.

"Hum... you smell so good!" she said kissing his mouth.

"You smell good too!" he replied kissing her back.

The two excited each other and ended up having sex, loving each other very carefully trying to give as much pleasure as possible to the other.

Mary snuggled on Paul and closed her eyes. She slept immediately and Paul looked at her smiling.

"I love you, Mary!" he said softly. Mary didn't hear anything.

Paul left her asleep, turned off the light and went down for a snack. He wouldn't wake Mary, he knew she'd had a long day and she was exhausted.

He had a quick snack and when he was coming up, Mary appeared on the stairs.

"You woke up, sleepy!" joked Paul, "come and have a snack."

"I've already had something to eat, honey, thank you!" said Mary sweetly. "Before I came up, I stopped by my place, took a shower, and had a snack. I'm sorry I fell asleep."

"Forget it! Have you relaxed a little?"

"Yes. Yes, I've rested. We can stay here and talk if you want," she said, already sitting on the big couch in the living room.

"Sure, we can! Would you like a glass of wine?"

"That would be great, Paul, thank you!"

Paul took the wine and the glasses and they sat comfortably on the couch.

"Honey, am I cleared to drive again? I need to get my life back on track in the office," he said looking at her.

"How do you feel?" she asked while taking a sip of her wine.

"I'm fine and ready."

"So, that's all right then. Avoid sudden braking and any kind of crashes!" this last recommendation came with a wink to him.

"Thank goodness Wagner provided me with another car while I was in the hospital."

"Did the insurance company call?"

"Yes. It was a total loss anyway. How did I survive it?" he looked into her eyes.

"I think you enjoy living," she said with a smile.

"Yes, but I don't understand. The crash was so destructive."

"You survived because you fought for your life, Paul, and those who fight for life often succeed."

"Sometimes, I had the impression of hearing your voice far away," he said.

"Yes. I talked to you all the time, I told you all about my life." she laughed.

"I'll remember everything, for sure," he said, smiling and drinking his wine.

"Hard to say, you were in an induced coma and I find it practically impossible for you to remember."

"Mary... I felt your love for me and I fought for you," he said hugging her. "Thank you so much, dear, for having fought for me so hard."

"I love you, Paul. I go crazy just thinking about losing you."

"You won't lose me, dear," he said kissing her head.

"I know," she closed her eyes and savored that moment of being close to him and thanked God.

The two finished their wine and went to bed. The next day would be a lot of work for both of them.

Debby arrived punctually at 3:30 p.m. and the doorman warned him she was coming up.

"Good afternoon, Paul!" said Debby giving him a kiss on his cheek.

"Good afternoon, darling! Thank you for coming," he said with a smile.

"What don't I do for you, huh?"

"So, let's sit over there on the balcony and organize everything," Paul said anxiously.

They talked for almost an hour and Debby stood up

smiling and confident.

"I hope you don't forget, Debby," he said looking at her seriously.

"Of course I won't! No way!" she smiled from ear to ear.

"Give me her mother's address now and I'll go there right away. I'll be out anyway and Mary's busy with her surgeries." they laughed, scheming behind Mary's back.

Paul gave her the address, thanked Debby for everything and saw her to the door.

"Thank you, darling! I mean it!" said Paul moved.

"It's going to be beautiful and very romantic. You men are great at catching us by surprise," she laughed and went to the elevator.

Paul finished his pleadings and an appeal that would have expired if he hadn't been to the office the day before. No one had remembered it.

Missing deadlines was bad for any lawyer and Paul had never let a deadline expire.

He decided to order a delicious lasagna for them to dine.

"Good evening, darling!" he greeted Mary as soon as she entered his apartment.

"Wow!! What's all this?" she asked in awe.

Paul had set a very elegant table; he even remembered to put flowers in a vase.

"I felt like surprising you with something beautiful," he smiled, hugging Mary who smelled fresh.

He kissed her passionately and without resisting each

other, they made love, took another shower, and went to dinner.

Paul felt happy and fulfilled.

"Time passes so fast!" Mary said.

"What do you mean?"

"Honey, Wagner and Debby's wedding is two months away," said Mary with her eyes wide opened. Paul laughed at her and said:

"Have you taken care of your bridesmaid dress yet?"

"I'm going to look at it today, in the break between one surgery and the other. I'm going to have a two-hour break, so I'm going to rush to take a look at the new dresses."

"My suit is already being made and if all goes well, I will have it in a few days."

"Wagner and Debby make a beautiful couple," Mary commented. "Have you seen them?"

"No!" was Paul's answer. He didn't tell her that Debby had been to his house that day.

They carried on with dinner and then Mary helped Paul wash the dishes and put them away. *We form a beautiful duo,* Mary thought.

Chapter Fifteen

The big day had finally arrived.

Mary and Paul were already placing themselves along with the other best men and bridesmaids. The wedding planner was giving the instructions to all of them.

"Mom! What a pleasant surprise! I had no idea you'd be here." Mary said when she spotted her elegantly dressed mother in a long dark blue dress, so beautiful.

"Good evening, darling!" her mother replied, hugging Mary and kissing her gently on the cheek. She greeted Paul with a hug and a kiss too.

"That's it then!" She gave a naughty smile.

Mary was glad to see her mother there but did not understand who invited her, and since she did not wish to be unkind, she decided not to ask any questions.

Wagner and Debby would have Wagner's two daughters as bridesmaids and Mark would enter the church side by side with his father.

First, all the best men and bridesmaids came coupled.

Alternating between one side of the altar and the other. Each couple would sit, forming a whole six couples—three on each side. Mary and Paul were the third couple to enter and everyone thought they were perfect.

All the best men were dressed alike, and the women each were each wearing a different color. Mary was in a beautiful dress of magnificent green, bringing out her beautiful green eyes.

Wagner walked in with his son, Mark, and that was a beautiful scene to see.

Debby was just breathtaking!

"What a beautiful bride!" That's what everyone was murmuring when they saw her come in arm-in-arm with her brother, Jason, as her father had already passed away.

The wedding was beautiful and the priest's words touched the hearts of all present.

Mary cried the whole wedding.

The reception was given in a huge space with live music and lots of laughter. The music was interrupted and everyone stopped to see the musician who was tapping the microphone with his fingers so that everyone would look at the stage.

"Attention! Attention!" called the singer into the microphone. Everyone stopped and looked at him, "now the bride will toss the bouquet, and she asks that all the single women stay here near the stage."

"Stand in the front, Mary, who knows you can catch the

bouquet and hook this wonderful man." her mother said smiling and winking at her.

"That's what I'm going to do," said a beautiful, smiling Mary.

Paul was very nervous and Mary's mother spoke, holding on to his arm.

"It's going to be all right, son." she smiled nicely and squeezed Paul's arm.

He shook his head and smiled.

"Are they all here?" asked Debby smiling and looking at all the women.

"Yes!" they responded smiling and screaming.

"So, I'm going to toss this wonderful bouquet and whoever picks it up will be the next one to get married." Debby was talking and laughing. "Get ready, girls."

All the single women got together to try to get Debby's bouquet. She pretended she was going to toss the bouquet twice and didn't toss it and the girls screamed.

"Come on, toss it!" they screamed laughing their heads off.

Debby pretended she was going to toss it a third time and turned around to face the girls and went to meet Mary and handed over the bouquet. Mary was surprised, and at the same time, Paul knelt in front of her.

"Mary, my love, will you marry me?"

Paul was on his knees with a little open box with a magnificent engagement ring in it.

Mary brought her hands to her mouth and began to cry, looking at Paul. The crowed was thrown off by Paul's beautiful gesture as he was there on his knee.

"Yes... Yes... my love." Mary answered.

Paul got up to put the ring on Mary's finger and lifted her up in his arms, swirling with her on the dance floor. Everyone clapped their hands to the sound of hurray! "Hurray!"

Debby hugged Mary and they both smiled like fools. Wagner came and hugged his friend and everyone celebrated, the music resumed and they went off dancing together.

Wagner and Debby were also dancing and the happiness on their faces could be seen a mile away.

"How on Earth were you able to organize all this?" Mary was radiant with such happiness. "Is that why Mom's here?" she asked with a smile.

"Yes. I couldn't ask the love of my life to marry me without her mother present, could I?" He held her in his arms and the two kissed passionately.

"I want to have a lot of kids," Paul said smiling and teasing her.

"I want a lot of kids too." She laughed as she danced with him.

"Thank you, love! For being you." Paul was too moved.

Mary thought about her life and thanked God. She closed her eyes swirling on the dance floor with Paul and knew she would be very happy.

Paul hugged her tightly and whispered in her ear in a hoarse and passionate voice.

"I wish I'd make love to you now, my beautiful and sexy fiancée," he hugged and kissed close to her ear.

Mary had goosebumps from head to toe and sank more

and more into Paul.

"Honey, I'm hard," he said, moving away from Mary a little bit so as not to embarrass himself.

Mary smiled with happiness and joy to learn that Paul was all excited about her.

"I love you, my love!" said Mary kissing his lips.

"I love you. You're the love of my life." Paul replied, looking across her face and stopping his eyes on her beautiful lips.

They kissed and there they knew that the love between them would overcome any obstacles that might come ahead.

Paul's parents interrupted their dance to congratulate them.

"You couldn't make me happier, Mary!" Paul's mother said affectionately hugging Mary.

"I wish you both all the happiness," said Paul's father, hugging the two thrilled.

The days flew by and both Mary and Paul worked hard. Paul was involved in a major case and took work home every day.

Mary kept her apartment and slept at Paul's house. They had definitely found love.

"Honey, tomorrow I'm going to Chicago," Mary told Paul.

"Did something happen?" he asked, hugging Mary and giving her a kiss.

"I'm accompanying Sissy," she said thrilled.

"Dr. Moses is lucky to have you, Mary." He said, loving that extraordinary woman even more.

"I can't deny him anything, Paul. Besides being a father to me, I love them both as if they were really my parents.

"I know, baby. Do the best you can."

"I'll be back in two days if all goes well," she said kissing Paul.

"I'm going to miss you. I love you, Mary!" Paul said, hugging Mary and feeling his heart tighten that she was going to Chicago.

"I love you too, Paul! Never forget that." She told him sweetly.

Mary left early, she just kissed Paul and ran to his apartment to shower and pack a small suitcase. It would only be two days.

Moses had warned Mary that the nephew of a friend would travel with them on his plane.

"Do you mind, honey?" Moses asked Mary.

"No, Moses, it's all right." She replied willingly.

Mary and Sissy got on the plane and found out who they were going to travel with, not just the friend but three young men. They greeted them and kept to themselves.

The flight was going to last about two and a half hours. In the middle of the trip, one of the boys began to feel sick. He put his hand on his chest announcing he was feeling great pain in his arm and chest.

Mary quickly got up from her seat.

"Take a deep breath," Mary said to the young man, standing right next to his seat.

The flight attendant came in scared and asked what she could do to help.

"He has symptoms of a heart attack," Mary said worriedly.

"Should I call the pilot?" asked the lady playing with her hands nervously.

"Please do." replied the young man who was standing next to Mary.

The flight attendant knocked on the cockpit and the pilot looked through the peephole. He saw who it was and opened the door.

"What happened?" he asked at the door.

But before the flight attendant said anything, the two young men got up with two pistols, and the third, who pretended to be sick, got up and pushed Mary into a seat. Mary screamed and fell to the ground.

She tried to get up, but the boy put his foot on her thigh and said, "stay right there."

"Pay attention, all of you! This plane is being commandeered and if everyone behaves, nothing will happen. Otherwise, I'm going to start killing people, do you understand?" he spoke loud and clear and was already pushing the pilot away from the door and entering the cockpit.

"You're going to turn around and fly lower so we don't get caught by the radar. Any acts of heroism and you die so he takes over. HAVE I MADE MYSELF CLEAR?" he shouted.

"I get it." said the pilot sweating, he was extremely nervous and shaking in fear as he answered.

Sissy was so terrified that she passed out.

"Can I check on my friend?" asked Mary.

"No!" was the short and rude answer.

"She's sick with cancer and she's not well, please,"

Mary begged.

"All right, but make it quick."

"Sissy. Sissy..." Mary patted her on the cheek and took her pulse. It was too weak.

"We need to land. She may die. Her pulse is very weak." Mary said, looking at them terrified.

The boys looked at one another and one of them said:

"If her time has come, she's going to die. We're not going to land anywhere."

"Can I get her some water?" Mary asked.

"Fine! But don't do anything funny, right?"

Mary just nodded that she had understood.

"Have some water, Sissy." Mary tried to revive Sissy, but she didn't look better.

"Do you have alcohol?" Mary asked the stewardess.

"We do," she answered shaking.

"Forget the beer. Get her some Scotch." Mary shook her head saying that would do.

The woman ran into the plane compartment and grabbed a small bottle of whiskey and handed it to Mary.

Mary put some whiskey in Sissy's mouth and made her swallow, holding her nose with two fingers.

Sissy coughed and opened her eyes.

"Calm down, dear, I'm here," said Mary meekly, holding her hand.

"What are they going to do with us, Mary?" asked Sissy terrified.

"I don't know, honey, let's wait."

Mary was shaking from head to toe. She knew that rarely would witnesses come out alive from a kidnapping.

She thought of her mother, Paul, and Moses as her eyes were filled with tears. Discreetly Mary stuck her hand in her coat pocket and put her cell phone in silent mode. She knew the last message she sent was for Paul and tried to remember how to get into the messages app without looking at the phone.

She didn't know if she was texting or what, but she wrote HEEEELP.

She couldn't tell if she wrote it right or not, or if at some point Paul would see it and if he would understand it. Nothing was certain.

She took her hand out of his pocket discreetly and stood next to Sissy, holding her hand.

Chapter Sixteen

The plane had already turned and Mary couldn't tell where they were going.

She prayed that there was internet on Moses' plane and that the message would reach Paul.

The tension was high on the plane, and Mary asked Sissy to remain calm so everything would be fine, but even she wasn't sure of it herself.

They were losing altitude and soon they would be landing. Mary wasn't sure of anything and felt distressed.

Meanwhile, at the hospital.

Knock... Knock... Knock.

"Come in," Moses answered by raising his head and staring at Mary's assistant.

"Excuse me, Dr. Moses," said the woman at the door.

"Yes. Any problems?" he asked rising from his chair.

"I don't know, Dr. Moses, I got this message from Dr. Taylor and I don't know what to do." the girl was talking as she showed Moses her phone.

HEEEELP.

"When was that?" he asked worriedly.

"It was a short time ago, as I was busy I didn't look at the phone. It was about an hour ago." She said looking at Moses in the eye.

"Then they were already flying," Moses said thoughtfully.

"I think so."

"I'll try to find out what's going on, thanks!" Moses sat down and became worried. He decided to call the airport to see if the plane had taken off all right.

"Yes, Dr. Moses. There were three young men as well. It took off properly and on time."

"I didn't know there were going to be three men," Moses said to the man in the control tower, who had been his friend for many years. "Is there any way you can communicate with the plane?"

"Sure, there is. I'll get in touch with them right now and get back to you."

"Thank you, Javier." Moses hung up and called Paul.

"Hello!"

"Paul, how're you? This is Moses," he said in a hurry.

"Are you all right? Did anything happen?" Paul noticed concern in the doctor's voice.

"Mary's assistant got a message from her asking for help. Did you get anything?"

Paul froze from head to toe.

"No," he said apprehensively. "Are you sure about that?"

"I've contacted the airport control tower and they will contact the plane and we will know in a little while. I will get back to you with more news."

"Thank you. Please, let me know as soon as you find out what is going on. I'll be waiting."

Paul said goodbye to Moses and leaned back in his office chair and felt a pang in his heart.

"My God, please forbid anything bad happens to Mary." He said a prayer silently and closed his eyes.

"Hello," Moses answered on the first tone.

"Dr. Moses, we're out of communication with the plane, and it's not on the radar. They must be flying very low and it's impossible to reach the pilot or flight attendant."

"Oh God! I don't understand, Javier."

"Do you know the three men who went with them?" asked the man on the other end of the line, showing concern.

"No. A friend asked to give his nephew a ride. I didn't know there were going to be three; I thought it was just his nephew. I'm going to call my friend and find out more. I'll get in touch as soon as I can."

Meanwhile, on the plane.

"Cher," called one of the boys who had tied the pilot and the flight attendant.

"Yes, everything all right?" the other man asked looking up.

"Someone here sent a warning," he said looking at Mary.

"What do you mean?" asked the other man nervously.

"The tower tried to communicate with us."

"Give me your cell phone," the man asked the pilot.

"It's in the cockpit." He answered while tied up.

"Where's yours?" he asked the stewardess.

"Mine is in the bag inside the luggage compartment on the left." she said frightened.

"YOU… Where's your cell phone?" he looked furiously at Mary.

Mary didn't answer his question.

The boy felt around Mary's coat pocket and took her cell phone. He shook her phone in front of her and said:

"Pray you didn't warn anyone, you slut. TELL ME THE PASSWORD," the man cried.

Mary was startled and told him the password. *We're now in God's hands*, she thought, lowering her head and praying.

Sissy was shaking terrified.

"She called for help," the man showed it to the other.

"You slut!" said the man slapping Mary in the face with all his might. She fell from the seat so hard was the slap. "I warned you, didn't I? " he took the gun and pointed at Mary's head.

Mary began to tremble all over and shrank terrified.

"Cher?" called the other one, "leave it, they can't track us, we're almost landing, and we're not killing anyone today."

The man pulled the gun from Mary's head and she breathed relieved crying. Before that, he kicked Mary in the belly, and she let out a cry of pain. Mary was stamped on her face; the slap had been so violent that the mark of the back of the man's hand remained. It was aching a lot and it started to swell.

Mary touched her face and looked at Sissy. She was crying too.

There was nothing they could do.

The plane landed on a dirt runway by a farm; there were only weeds and bushes. Mary didn't know where they were. The runway was short, and the pilot had to juggle so that the landing was made without anyone getting hurt.

Two of them got off the plane and picked up a radio. They spent a long time talking there.

"All right," said a tall man to the one who was keeping an eye on the passengers.

"Let's go down. Hurry up!" he said, already grabbing Sissy by the arm and raising her rudely. She staggered and he screamed, "DON'T PLAY THE VICTIM. Move... Move..."

Sissy was scared and Mary went along to hold her hand and help her down the stairs.

The flight attendant was also released and was taken along with Mary and Sissy. Just the pilot and the co-pilot remained on the plane.

The armed man told them to go into the woods and they obeyed, tripping over branches and Sissy fell once, but Mary helped her. They were being treated like animals and Mary was terrified because Sissy's health was very delicate.

They arrived in a cabin in the middle of the woods and the boy pushed the flight attendant for her to open the cabin.

"Open the door, MOVE!" cried the man.

The flight attendant was shaking from head to toe and couldn't get the key in the lock. The man struck her on the head, throwing the girl to the side causing her to fall and Sissy screamed.

"SHUT UP, YOU OLD FOOL! COME ON IN, QUICK!" he shouted, ordering them loudly.

The hut was a real fortress, all gridded and with thick and very firm woods. The man pushed them in as the other man arrived with their belongings, except for their cell phones. He threw everything on the floor, and they left and locked the big wooden door from the outside.

As soon as Mary saw that they were no longer there, she tried to open the door and she noticed they would never be able to open that door.

"And now, Mary, what are we going to do?" Sissy asked trembling and crying terrified.

"The first thing to do is remain calm and think about a way out. It's no use crying."

"What's your name?" she asked the flight attendant, who wouldn't stop crying.

"Brenda, Brenda Smith."

"Brenda, please stop crying or you're going to have a huge headache," Mary said nicely. "It's no use crying, let alone be agitated. Let's try to get out of here to warn someone." Mary said as she looked around the cabin.

"We have no idea where we are," Brenda said, cleaning her eyes and blowing her nose on her handkerchief.

"That's true." Mary kept trying to find a solution. She decided to check the rest of the cabin.

There were supplies for at least a week. There was very

little later, so they would have to save it because they could run out of it. This was a sign that they were prepared to leave them there for a long time. She became worried. There was nowhere to take a shower and there was a place inside the cabin, which was just a hole with a board on top. There they would have to satisfy their bathroom needs but almost no toilet paper.

"I'm going to be very frank with you because I have to. We need to save water, toilet paper, and food. Based on the amount of food they left for us, they intend to leave us here for some time, maybe a week, I don't know. That spot over there, that's where we're going to go for a bathroom."

Sissy began to cry and Mary hugged her.

"Honey, you need to be strong now," Mary said calmly, patting her on her back. "Surely someone has received my distress call and they are already after us."

"I hope you're right, Mary," Sissy said in a sad voice.

Paul was terrified when he got to the hospital and rushed to Moses' office. Moses was walking from side to side like a caged nervous animal.

"Take a seat, Paul," Moses said, taking his cell phone from his ear. "I'm trying to talk to my friend. He is the uncle of the man who went with them to Chicago."

Moses was waiting for his friend to get his phone, he was playing golf and the caddy told him he would take the device to him.

"What's up, Moses? Is everything all right?" his friend said cheerfully.

"David, any news from your nephew? Have they arrived in Chicago yet?" asked Moses terrified.

"What nephew? I don't understand, Moses. Is everything okay?"

Moses sat down whiter than snow with his mouth open.

"Moses, are you there?" said his friend on the other side of the line. Paul noticed Moses' shock and took the cell phone from his hand. Moses had his eyes scarred and was completely motionless.

"Hello, this is Paul. My fiancée was on the plane with your nephew. We want to know if they've made it to Chicago fine."

"I don't understand Paul," David said. "I don't know which of my nephews went to Chicago."

"I don't understand," Paul said. "I'm going to pass it on to Moses. Moses, please." Paul said shaking Moses.

Moses came out of the trance and took the phone from Paul's hand. He was shaking a lot.

"David? Didn't you ask me to give your nephew a ride on my jet?" Moses asked a little louder.

"No! My nephews have no business in Chicago. What's going on, Moses?" asked his friend worried.

"Thank you, David. I'll talk to you later." Moses hung up his cell phone and looked at Paul.

"Now what?" said Paul waiting for an answer.

"Paul, I think there's been a big mistake and I've got them all in trouble."

"Tell me everything, please." Paul was very worried and needed to get something out of Moses.

"David called me, now I know it wasn't him, and asked if I could take his nephew to Chicago on my jet since he had business there. Moses was very deep as he told Paul the story. "I don't know what happened, Paul."

The phone rang and Moses answered.

"Hello, it hasn't arrived? Oh, God. Yes, we'll be waiting."

"What was that?"

"The plane may have been hijacked; it hasn't landed at any airport."

"I'm going to call my dad. He's a retired officer." Paul said as he picked up his phone and called his father.

Paul and his father talked for twenty minutes. He told his father everything he knew about the case, asking Moses some questions every now and then.

"Yes. They were to have arrived three hours ago. Thank you, Dad."

 said Paul nervously. "Sure, I tell him." He hung up and looked at Moses.

"Most likely, they were really kidnapped," said Paul devastated and miserable.

Moses sat down, shaken and devastated.

He was in a state of shock.

"Moses, is there anyone I can call to keep you company while I go to my parents' house?" asked Paul worried about him due to his age.

"Don't worry, Paul, I'll start praying, and God will bring back our women, safe and sound," he said looking into his eyes.

"I'll keep you posted."

"Thank you, Paul."

Chapter Seventeen

Paul was with his father at his house. He walked in circles, not knowing where or who to turn to. His father was on the phone.

"Calm down, son! Everything will be all right," his mother said, giving him a glass of lemonade.

"Mom, I can't lose the love of my life." Paul sat on the couch and cried.

His mother sat next to him on the arm of the couch and hugged him. "It's going to be all right, honey, have a little more faith."

Paul got up without touching the lemonade, his stomach was upset, and he didn't want to eat or drink. He wanted Mary.

"Please, God, take care of Mary." he prayed while his father was on the phone with someone from the FBI.

"Okay, let me know if anything comes up. Thank you so much, Will." His father hung up and turned to Paul.

"What now, Dad?" he asked with his eyes red and wide open.

"Sit down, Paul. Let's talk." his father was serious and very concerned.

"According to Will, who works for the FBI, there's a group of radicals involved in terrorist acts here in the United States. He can't tell me what group this is. They hijack small planes that can be landed in forests and small roads. No matter if the crew members are saved or not. They've been after this group for a long time, but they're smart and haven't made any mistakes so far."

"So what do we do now?" Paul asked, even more distressed and frightened.

"He's going to make some calls and make other arrangements, Paul. We need to stay calm and wait."

"Dad, Mary is with them." Paul was really desperate. His parents looked at each other and his father said:

"If you don't calm down, you'll end up having a heart attack. This may last for days, Paul," his father spoke trying to calm him down."

"And until then, what can we do?"

"Nothing! Nothing! We wait for Will to call us. He will do it as soon as he hears anything. Now it is in God's hands."

"I'll stay here with you," he said sadly, taking a sip of his lemonade.

Mary was looking for a way out of that situation, but the cabin was very well made and seemed to be made of steel. The wood was thick and solid. She decided to check what was in the cabin and was disappointed to find that there were no sharp objects in the cabin.

They didn't leave a knife there, so they couldn't pierce the boards.

"Think Mary... think," she spoke internally.

It was late in the afternoon and Mary and Brenda got the three of them something to eat. They saved as much water as possible for fear there wouldn't be enough.

They went to bed early since there was nothing to do. They were locked and isolated. There were only two beds and Mary slept on a sofa that was too small for her.

They had been locked up for three days and no bath. Sissy had been sick and Mary did everything to make her more comfortable.

"Take that bowl and fill it with water, Brenda. Not too much water as we need to save it."

Mary gave Sissy a sponge bath to make her fresher, the heat was unbearable and there was only a small window very high in the wall with solid grids. No one could reach it climbing up the chair.

"Brenda, I've got an idea; maybe it'll work," Mary said looking at her.

"Go ahead, tell us, doctor, I'll do whatever it takes."

"I'm going to squat and you're going to climb up on my shoulders and hold on to the wall, so you don't fall. Let's see if you can see out there and update us on how the situation is. Take a good look if there's anyone out there, right?"

"OK."

Mary went under the window and lowered facing the wall. She needed to lean on the wall too as not to fall.

Brenda leaned on Mary and climbed on her shoulders, but as there was nothing to hold, she fell four times.

"We're not giving up, Brenda." Mary said hopefully.

"I can help." Sissy said, standing up slowly and very weak and holding Brenda's hand holding the other against the wall.

"Are you sure you can do it, Sissy?" Mary asked apprehensively.

"I can do it," she answered weakly.

With great difficulty, Mary managed to get up and Brenda held firmly on the window bars, she stretched which hurt Mary's shoulder, but she said nothing.

"What do you see, Brenda?" asked Mary breathlessly.

"There's no one out there, not even a car, but I can see a light at a distance. It must be far away because it's very weak."

"OK. I'm going to get down so you can come down and the three of us are going to think of something."

Mary started lowering slowly so Brenda could come down and always holding Sissy's hand.

"All right, let's see if there's any possibility we can break through the floor, I mean, make an opening somewhere so I can go out and get help."

"I think it's too risky, Mary," said Sissy wringing her hands.

"If anyone comes, we're dead. These people are no joke."

"Either we're all going, or nobody's going," Brenda said.

"OK. OK, let's come up with a plan then."

Meanwhile, elsewhere, there were at least twenty-five people working with large amounts of C4, being used to make bombs and the plane would be used as transportation. One of the three boys would die with the pilot; that was very clear because the plane would be thrown into some building in the city. All three volunteered to go. They weren't afraid of dying.

The pilot and the co-pilot were terrified. They had families and didn't want to die.

They were both being held at gunpoint.

The people in the shed made bombs, bomb vests, and many other things to be used in places with large crowds of tourists.

The hijacked plane would serve to take them from one place to another, and at the end of the mission, they would launch themselves into some building.

The goal was to make as many victims as possible and terrify people.

The work to do evil was intense and there was no respite.

Brenda found a spoon that might serve to dig a hole, it would take a long time because the spoon was small, but if they didn't try they would die there.

Mary chose a place to make the hole that they could hide with some furniture in case anyone showed up.

Sissy was not in a condition to make any effort. Mary would never let her anyways. Mary tore one of her dresses that was inside her little suitcase and made a dressing for herself and Brenda's hands, so they wouldn't grow blisters preventing them from digging.

They started drilling through the floor near a basket that was left in a corner. The land was very hard, and the water was too little to be wasted watering the earth.

She and Brenda couldn't dig anything with the spoon, it was too small and soon it got all twisted.

Mary was desperate because she knew they'd die in there; if it wasn't for starvation, it'd be dehydration. She knew no one would come back to free them.

Everything she thought didn't work out. She was starting to lose hope and there was nothing in the cabin they could use to break free.

"Brenda, what's the window like? Did you find it was too hard?"

"I don't know, doctor, I didn't get a chance to look. I just held the bars, which were iron. There's no way to break them."

"Start looking at every corner of this cabin Brenda, I'll do the same. See if you can find something we can use to get out of here."

"OK," answered the girl, already rummaging through everything.

"I didn't find anything," she said after a while.

"Neither did I." they looked at Sissy who was asleep.

"What's the bed made of? " asked Mary coming closer to the bedside.

Brenda looked and said, "It's iron."

"Maybe we can take it apart and use a piece of it. What do you think?"

"It may work," replied the girl hopefully.

"Let's wait for Sissy to wake up and take the bed apart,"

Mary said worried about Sissy.

"Is she going to be okay?" Brenda asked softly.

"She's a strong woman and she might make it, but I can't promise anything, she's taken too much medication and she's weak."

"You can give her my share of the food, Doctor. I can keep myself out of food for two days." She said.

"Thank you, Brenda. I hope I don't have to do that."

Mary liked the solidarity of such a young woman and admired her for it.

Finally in the late afternoon, Sissy woke up and Mary fed her what she thought was best because there were not many options and nothing was hot.

The food they left was all prefabricated. Either they ate cold food or didn't eat at all.

"Sit down over there, dear," said Mary affectionately.

"Let's take the bed apart to see if we can find anything, Brenda."

 Said Mary, already taking out the mattress.

They looked at the whole bed and decided to remove one of the iron bars, so they could pierce the floor or try to open the door; it was all useless. The bar was no good and Mary didn't know what else to do.

They've been locked there for seven days by Mary's account.

"Let's go to bed. Now there's no point trying anything else. It's getting dark and we won't be able to see anything else."

"We'll try something first thing in the morning," said Mary

feeling tired.

"All right, Dr. Taylor," Brenda said.

"Please, Brenda, switch beds with Sissy. She won't endure getting down to lie on the mattress on the floor." Mary said looking at Sissy and feeling sorry for her, who was increasingly thinner and weaker.

The next day, Mary called Brenda to get back to work to try a way out. Sissy was asleep.

"Let's try the door again. Maybe we'll find a way to open it."

Mary analyzed the door lock and didn't know anything about locks. But she had an idea. "Let's try to get the cylinder out and see what happens." She spoke hopefully.

With great difficulty and after two hours trying to unscrew the four screws, with the crooked spoon and some broken nails, dirty and sweaty, she and Brenda managed to remove the cylinder and started pushing the latch with a very small piece of iron, which was part of the bed.

Five hours later, exhausted and with their hands and fingers all injured, the two women finally managed to open the door.

"Thank God!" said Sissy.

"Sissy, do you think you can walk? We don't know what's out there or if we will be able to find anything."

"I'm going to try Mary. With God's help, I'm going to try."

They inhaled the fresh air of the forest and Mary raised her eyes to the sky, thanking God and asking for protection.

"Brenda, let's get some sheets and tie them to our shoulder and waist and make some kind of bag to bring food and water. We can't leave empty-handed."

The two women tied a piece of cloth to Sissy so she could take light things such as their coats. Mary and Brenda took the only bottle of water and all the food that was in the cabin, which was very little, and Mary also took an iron rod from the bed and gave one to Brenda in case they found any predators. They needed to defend themselves.

The three women began to walk in the direction of the sun, but the night would come fast and they didn't even have a flashlight, nothing to lighten the night.

They kept walking hoping to find a road and they had already been walking for about four hours when Sissy sat on a rock and said:

"Mary?" called Sissy breathless, "I'm very tired and I'm not going to make it. You and Brenda go ahead. I'm going to stay behind waiting for help."

Mary looked into the woods and she would never leave Sissy there alone.

"No. Let's get some rest, have something to eat, and move on. The road is not far away, I'm sure of it."

They picked up the water and some food and ate, leaving most of the food to Sissy.

As they were getting ready to leave, two armed men showed up.

The three women got scared and were curled up clinging to each other, not knowing how to react to the two strangers.

"What are you guys doing here?" One of the men asked,

pointing the gun at them.

"We are fleeing, we have been kidnapped, and we were locked in a cabin. Please help us, you will be well rewarded." Mary said desperately.

The second man looked right at Mary, who was dirty and disheveled, but recognized her immediately.

"Are you Dr. Taylor?" he said lowering the gun.

"Yes, that's me. Do you know me?" she asked relaxing a little.

The man lifted up his shirt and showed a large scar on his belly on the right side.

"You saved me and took care of me in the hospital when I was shot. We're here to help you."

Mary began to cry compulsively and threw herself on the man's feet thanking him. She was having a breakdown.

The man picked her up, hugged her and said:

"Don't worry, Doc, I'm going to repay you for everything you did for me. You fought for my life and I will fight for yours. The time to give back has come."

"Hurry, before someone shows up!" said the other man helping Sissy, who was very weak.

As Sissy could no longer walk, the man asked permission and placed her on his shoulder upside down.

"Just for a little while, our truck's right over there on the other side."

Sissy was carried until they got to the car and they laid her down over a piece of canvas in the back of the pick-up truck.

Mary and Brenda sat in the front squeezed with the two men.

Chapter Eighteen

"As soon as there's a signal, I'll give you my cell phone so you can communicate with the family." said John, the man Mary had saved.

"Thank you so much, John. I don't know how to thank you for that."

As soon as they hit the road and they got a signal, the man stopped the truck on the side of the road and handed the phone to Mary. Mary typed the numbers, still shaking.

"Hello!" answered Paul, his voice sounded anxious.

"Paul? It's me!" and she started crying.

"Mary? Where are you, my love?" Paul sounded nervous and terrified.

"Darling, thank God! We're fine, I'm going to pass the phone to John who rescued us in the woods, and he'll tell you where we are. Please, let Moses know we are all right. There is no time to talk," said Mary passing her phone to John.

"Good evening, yes. Oh, we are really very far from you, you'd better send a plane. The lady who's with them isn't well at all. I'll give you all the coordinates and we'll be there when you land."

"Thank you so much, John. You will be very well rewarded." Paul said.

"I don't want any money, sir. Many years ago, Dr. Taylor saved my life, and today fate made us come across each other so I can repay her. Don't worry, we'll take care of them."

"Thank you, my friend. You will always have my respect and my gratitude."

"Thanks a lot," John replied, quietly moved.

John gave Paul all the coordinates as to where the plane was supposed to land, a short, dirt runway in the middle of nowhere.

"Yes, it was pure luck to have found them. They would never survive alone in the woods. There are big wild animals there," John went on to explain to Paul.

Paul called Moses immediately.

"Moses?" Paul said excited. "Mary's just called, and we will need a plane or a helicopter to pick them up." Paul did not wait for Moses' replay and went on talking.

"I'm sorry." He heard a woman's voice, "this is Dr. Graham's cell phone. He had a heart attack yesterday morning and is in critical condition in the ICU. Who is it, please?"

"Oh my God! My name is Paul O'Brian and I'm Dr. Taylor's fiancé. She is with Moses' wife, Sissy."

"How are they, Mr. O'Brian?" She asked her, crying, "this is Judy. I've been working with Dr. Graham for twenty-five years."

"According to the person who spoke to me, Sissy's not well at all. She is very weak," answered Paul sadly. "I'm sorry about Moses."

"I'll arrange a large helicopter so you can go as well," said Judy with a voice changed by emotion. "Dr. Graham made it very clear that the top priority was to do everything possible to save both his wife and Dr. Taylor," said the very sad woman.

"Thank you, Judy! Everything is going to be all right," Paul said hanging up.

"Dad!" called Paul on his way to meet him.

His father reported to the FBI immediately and spent half an hour with them on the phone.

"Oh, thank God." Paul said hugging his father and his mother. Judy called and told him she had already got him a helicopter and Paul asked his father to accompany him, "I'm very shaken, Dad."

"Of course, I will go with you, son." Answered his father willingly already putting on the suit jacket.

"So, let's go to the airport." Paul said leaving already. While they were on their way to the airport, Paul called Mary's mother and told her news that he was on his way to pick them up.

"Yes. Everything is fine," he assured her. Mary's mother thanked him crying.

Paul hung up right as the phone rang.

"Hello," Paul answered and it was Judy.

"Mr. O'Brian? I don't. I have good news," She said

beginning to cry.

"What is it, Judy?" Paul was terrified and his father was driving to the airport as fast as he could.

"Dr. Graham had another heart attack and passed away. I'm sorry."

"Oh my God! We'd better not tell Sissy now. She's not well. Is there anyone you can call to make all the arrangements?" asked Paul devastated.

"I'll take care of everything myself because the emergency contact for both Dr. Graham and Sissy is Dr. Taylor."

"OK. I'm so sorry, Judy," Paul said.

"It's fine, thank you!" she hung up crying a lot. She'd known them for thirty years and loved them as if they were her parents. It will be very painful for Sissy, she thought still weeping. The two were so close.

"What happened, Paul?" his father asked as soon as Paul hang up.

"Moses has just passed away; he couldn't bear another heart attack." Paul was sad and had no idea how he was going to give Mary the news. Mary loved him like a father.

Paul's father held his hand, giving his son strength. They arrived as fast as they could and went straight to the runway.

The helicopter was big enough to carry six people. Since it was prepared to rescue hostages, it was equipped with first aid equipment.

"How are you?" greeted Paul shaking the pilot's hand.

"Can I have the coordinates the man gave you? I have to

report it to the tower and ask permission to take off."

"Here they are." Paul gave him everything and waited, walking nervously from side to side.

"Calm down, son! It's going to be all right." His father said walking behind Paul.

"Eight days, dad. I can't even imagine how they survived this, damned kidnappers!" Paul said angrily.

Sissy wasn't well, and Mary was very concerned about her health. She urgently needed to go to an ICU.

"John, I can't thank you enough!" said Mary taking the man's hand and crying once more.

She thought she was strong and could face any hardship, but eight days without showering, without eating properly, and dehydrated was too much for all of them.

"Everything will be fine, Dr. Taylor," said John. He was patient and his voice was calm and reassuring.

"Come and take a shower. It's going to be a while before they get there. There are some employee overalls over here if you don't mind wearing it," he said shyly. "They've been washed and ironed."

"I don't mind." She said gratefully.

Mary went to the bathroom of the small cabin in the middle of the forest and took a long and relaxing shower. John said there was no need to worry about the water because it came from the river and there was plenty of it.

Mary spent half an hour in the shower and thanked God for being alive. *I've lost a few pounds, but I'm alive,* she thought crying again.

"Brenda!" called Mary as she left the bathroom already cleaned and dressed in a brown men's jumpsuit. It was loose, but it was clean.

"Go take a shower, I'll find a way to bathe Sissy, will you help me?" asked Mary.

"Of course, Dr. Taylor, I'm going to take a shower and then I'll come and help you.

"Sissy, Sissy." called Mary.

But there was no answer. She was already going into a coma. Mary sobbed and Brenda reached and hugged her; she had already taken her shower and was wearing a jumpsuit as well.

"I don't think she's going to make it," Mary said crying. "Moses will be devastated," Mary wept for a long time, and they went to clean Sissy, who also wore a jumpsuit.

Sissy's pulse was too weak, and it was only a matter of hours before she passed away.

"Sissy, my dear, you're like a mother to me," Mary said crying and holding her hand. "I'm sorry I didn't think of opening that door before, I'm so sorry!" Mary wouldn't stop crying when John knocked on the door, warning that he could hear the sound of a helicopter.

"We'll come out of it, darling. Please hold on." Mary said sweetly and passed her hand on Sissy's arm that was already getting cold. She knew death was already lurking.

"The helicopter is about to land, Dr. Taylor," John said.

Mary left the house with Brenda right behind her and saw the powerful machine going down, imagining the pain Moses would feel.

"Mary!" Paul got out of the helicopter, hugging her tightly. "My love!" he said crying.

Mary also cried a lot and said:

"Where's Moses? He didn't want to come?"

Before Paul could answer, John came running.

"Dr. Taylor, there's something wrong with Sissy." Mary left Paul and ran into the cabin.

"Sissy," called Mary crying. "Don't leave me, Sissy. Stay with me." Mary cried desperately and Paul hugged her.

Sissy took her last breath.

"Oh, God, what am I going to tell Moses?" she cried and shook all over, squeezing Paul in her arms.

"Honey..." said Paul moving his hands on her back. They were alone in the hut.

"Yes." she noticed his voice, "Did anything happen?"

"Yes. Unfortunately, Moses had two heart attacks and passed away this morning." Mary hugged Paul, sobbing and understood that perhaps it was better for Sissy. She wouldn't fight cancer if she survived.

They went outside and Mary hugged Paul's father. He noticed how much thinner she was, but he didn't say a word.

They all helped to move Sissy's body. The time and day of death were written down and Mary was feeling miserable.

They took the helicopter back and Paul promised to repay

everything John did, despite the man's protest.

Mary was exhausted physically and mentally.

"Yes?" Judy answered Moses's cell phone.

"Judy, I'm afraid I don't have good news, either." Paul said.

"What happened, Mr. O'Brian?" her voice showed concern.

"Unfortunately, Sissy couldn't hold and died as well." He said affected.

"Oh my God! Even in death they were close," Judy was weeping.

"I'm sorry to give you the news like this, but we're almost there and I was wondering if you could send the funeral home to pick her up, so she and Moses can be cremated together."

"Is Dr. Taylor going to certify the death?" she asked, crying a lot.

"Yes. She'll do it. We'll drop by our home so that Mary can take a shower and change."

"All right! I never thought we'd have to do this. I'm so devastated." Judy said weeping.

"It's really very sad, Judy. My condolences to all of you." Paul hung up and hugged Mary, who was devastated and depressed.

"In the midst of all this," Paul's father said, "we have good news."

"What was that, Dad?" Paul asked looking at his father and shouting because of the noise.

"The kidnappers were all arrested. The FBI found out where they were based on the location of the cabin John gave them." Paul's father was glad. "By the amount of C4 they found, there was going to be mass causalities."

"Were all three arrested?" asked Mary.

"There were twenty-five people in all, Mary,"

Mary shook her head. She wasn't in the mood for hearing anything else.

Chapter Nineteen

Paul and Mary went home. Mary was in shock over the death of Moses and Sissy.

She still could not believe everything that had happened.

Paul walked with her into her apartment and from there, he ordered food for the two of them.

Mary took a shower, put on a comfortable outfit and laid down on her bed. She was very downcast and dreary.

"Honey!" he said sitting on the bed next to her. "Let's go to my place. I also need a good shower and the food will arrive in a few minutes. I don't want to leave you alone."

Mary nodded in agreement, he took her hand and they went to the penthouse together.

"Lie down here, honey. I'll be right back." He said to her very affectionately.

Mary lay down in bed with her eyes open. Paul took a quick shower and warned the doorman that Sharon, Mary's mother, was coming, that he should let her up.

The bell rang and he ran to open the door.

"Thank God you're here, Sharon. Mary's not doing too well."

"She loved Moses and Sissy very much, they had known her since she graduated, and they did everything for her."

"She didn't say a word, Sharon. I'm very worried. Do you think we should call a doctor?" asked Paul, not knowing what to do.

"No. Mary is like that; when she gets sad she keeps silent. Let's give her some time to grieve, and if it's necessary we intervene."

"Please, come up, darling. I'm waiting for the food I ordered to see if she eats something. I think she'll be happy to see you."

Sharon went upstairs and stood by the door watching her frail daughter lying on Paul's king-size bed.

"Mary." She came closer and Mary got up and sat on the bed. She hugged her mother crying and sobbing, moving her body back and forth.

"Calm down, honey. I'm here. Calm down."

Mary shed some tears and was much calmer, her mother was what she needed, and Paul was wonderful in calling her.

"I'm so shaken and sad, Mom. How on Earth did we lose them both! In one day? I don't understand that."

"But I do," said her mother looking into Mary's eyes and taking her hand.

"How come," Mary asked with red eyes, swollen and wide-open, "you understand?" asked Mary.

"Honey, Moses and Sissy's love existed beyond physical.

They loved each other with their souls and spirits. Their involvement was more spiritual than carnal. Do you think they could survive away from each other? I'm sure they couldn't."

"Okay, you've got a point." Mary thought about it and saw that her mother was right.

"God did Moses a favor. You can be sure of that! Sissy would not live too long with her health as it was. And you know that, right?" Her mother looked at her.

"Yes. Her strength was very fragile, and she was already suffering from nausea and other things. She didn't know, but she was already metastasized."

"So darling, she was full of life. She didn't just deserve to die. They are together and happy now, I'm sure of it," said her mother.

"Thank you, Mom!" Mary hugged her mother.

"Let's go down, honey. Paul doesn't deserve this. He's worried and ordered some food."

"All right, you go ahead, and I will come down after," said Mary beginning to accept the situation.

Sharon left and Mary planted her feet out of bed. She'd have to react and accept her friend's death.

"I love you both, my darlings, and I will never forget you. You will always be in my heart. See you one day, dears" Mary said moved.

"Mary!" called Paul standing up to hug her. "How are you feeling?" He was caring and careful.

"I'm feeling better, darling. Thank you for calling Mom."

Mary hugged him and kissed him on his lips.

"I love you, Mary!" Paul said, touching his forehead against hers.

"I love you too, my love," she spoke emotionally.

As she hugged Paul, she felt that he had lost a lot of weight as well.

The food arrived and Paul set the table with three plates.

Mary found out she was hungry, and it was great to have eaten hot, tasty food.

"Are you satisfied?" asked Paul putting his hand on hers.

"I am," Mary said sweetly.

They talked a little, avoiding at all costs to mention the kidnapping and death of their friends.

Mary was exhausted and getting sleepy. Paul suggested she went to bed and Sharon offered to keep her company until she fell asleep.

After putting Mary to bed and giving her a kiss, he prepared the guest room for Sharon and went down to call his parents.

"Mom," said Paul acknowledging his mother's voice immediately.

"I was so worried, honey. How's Mary?" His mother asked.

"I called Sharon to spend the night here and Mary seems to be better after she saw her mother. She managed to eat a little and now she is in the bedroom."

"That's good, Paul! I was very worried about all this. Thank God it is all over," said his mother.

"Can I talk to Dad?" Paul asked.

"I'll get him," said his mother saying goodbye to Paul with so many recommendations that it would be impossible to keep them all.

"Paul?" said his father.

"Dad, how is everything? What did the kidnappers say?" Paul asked anxiously.

"Will told me he can't comment on the operation with me." His father said ending the conversation.

"OK."

"Son, the damage would have been enormous had they used all the stockpile they found in the hut."

"I can imagine, though I don't understand anything about it."

"When's the funeral?" asked his father changing the subject.

"Tomorrow at 10:00 a.m."

"We'll be there."

Paul said goodbye to his father and went to take a look at Mary, she was asleep, and her mother was sitting in an armchair near her in Paul's bedroom.

"Come, let's talk a little, Sharon," Paul whispered to her. She nodded and left the room.

They both went down and went to the balcony.

"Would you like a glass of wine?" Paul asked politely.

"Yes, please. Thank you!"

Paul poured the wine and sat in a comfortable armchair facing Sharon.

"It's very beautiful here, Paul. What a wonderful view!"

"Yes. That's what attracted me most to this penthouse."

"Tomorrow Mary will have a difficult day," she said thoughtfully.

"Yes. She loved them very much."

"As you know, Paul, I raised Mary alone and we've been through a lot of difficulties. She met Moses before she even thought about being a doctor. I think, in a way, Moses influenced her in the profession. He called her to work at the hospital and still did not own part of it, much less being the director. He was an extremely competent surgeon and Mary learned a lot from him."

"They didn't have any children?" asked Paul taking a sip of his wine.

"No. Sissy had endometrial cancer and had to remove it all. That's how they met. He fell in love with the patient."

Sharon smiled as she recalled this moving story. "They really loved each other very much." There were tears in her eyes.

"Mary said the same." He said.

"Mary was like a daughter to Moses. They loved her, too," said Sharon finishing her wine.

"I'm going to bed, Paul. It's been a long day. Thank you for everything!" Sharon smiled at Paul and stood up.

"I love your daughter and that's never going to change."

"I know, and she loves you, too. Good night!

"Good night, Sharon."

The new day was sad and gray.

Chapter Twenty

Mary opened her eyes and looked at Paul sleeping beside her. *He's a lot thinner*, she thought.

She got up slowly so as not to wake him. She put on her slippers and went down. She found her mother looking for a frying pan to make bacon and eggs.

"You're up already, Mom?" Mary asked coming closer to her mother to kiss her.

"Good morning! How did you spend the night?" her mother asked staring at her.

"It was a night full of nightmares and a lot of sadness, but I was able to sleep. I was very tired." Mary replied sweetly and very shaken.

"I think it was better that way, don't you? Moses would not survive without Sissy." Her mother said as she put the scrambled eggs and bacon on the plate for Mary.

"Mom, I don't think I can eat," she said.

"Try to eat a little, dear. I'll prepare some for Paul too." her mother spoke, smiling at Mary.

Sharon was calm, sweet and passed all this on to Mary. The atmosphere was quiet, and Mary ate everything without even realizing it.

"Thank you, Mom," Mary said hugging her mother.

"Good morning!" Paul entered the kitchen, gave Mary a kiss on the lips and one on Sharon's cheek.

"Good morning!" They answered.

"How did you spend the night, honey?" Paul asked, noticing that Mary was too thin.

"I had a good night, even though I'm very shaken by all this."

"It's normal, darling." He hugged her and kissed her head.

"I'm going home to get ready for the funeral," Mary said and walked away.

"Mary," Her mother called, "wait till I finish here and I'll go with you."

"Don't worry about it, Sharon, I'll finish here. Go keep Mary company. She needs you." Paul was understanding and sensitive to Mary's feelings.

"Thank you, Paul!" said Sharon, following Mary.

They were ready and Paul stopped by Mary's apartment for the three of them to go down together.

The funeral was sad and there was a good amount of people there. Everyone was sorry and surprised by their passing on the same day.

Few people participated in the cremation, but Mary was there.

"The hospital will never be the same without Moses." thought Mary weeping.

Paul was there for Mary and was distressed by her pain. After everyone got home, Mary's phone rang.

"Yes!" answered Mary not recognizing the number.

"Good afternoon, Dr. Taylor!" spoke the voice of an older man.

"Good afternoon! Who is it?"

"My name is Douglas Simpson and I'm Dr. Stewart's lawyer and administrator.

"Okay! How I can help you, Mr. Simpson?"

"We need to talk. Will you be in the hospital tomorrow, or will you stay home?" He asked politely.

"Tomorrow I will not go to the hospital, if you want, you can come to my apartment, if it is very important," said Mary who was still very sad.

"It's really important," he said. "Please, let me have your address and what time we can meet."

Mary talked to him a little more trying to find out what the administrator might want from her.

"Tomorrow, I'll explain everything, have a nice day."

"Is everything all right, my love?" asked Paul by pouring them some lemonade.

The two of them were alone. After the funeral, Sharon had returned to her home.

"I don't know, honey, Moses' lawyer and administrator want to talk to me."

"Moses must have left some instruction for it. Do you want me to be there? As a lawyer?" he asked willingly.

"Thank you, dear, you don't have to."

"If anything happens, I'll be in the office and you can call me, okay?" He said hugging Mary.

"Thank you, Paul!" Mary was too moved.

The next day, Mary went to her apartment to wait for Mr. Simpson and Paul went to his office.

"You can let him in, thank you!"

"Good morning Mr. Simpson," greeted Mary shaking the lawyer's hand.

"Good morning!" he replied politely. She's really very shaken, Douglas thought, noticing Mary's sad face.

"Let's sit here at the table," Mary said. "What can I do for you?"

"Dr. Taylor..."

"Please, call me Mary." she interrupted him.

"All right. Call me Douglas." He said with a sad smile.

Mary stared at the man's face, who appeared to be about the same age as Moses.

"Mary, a few years ago, Moses made a will. I wrote it myself and Sissy was in total agreement with it."

"Yes," Mary answered, but she couldn't understand anything.

"We're going to do the reading today at 4:00 p.m. However, since you're the only beneficiary, I think it's ok if I assume it goes to you. What do you think?"

"I'm not sure I understand, Douglas. Did Moses leave everything to me?"

Mary was taken by surprise.

"Not only did he leave something to you, but he also left everything he had." He spoke with professionalism.

"I don't get it," said Mary still confused.

"Mary, as you are well aware, they didn't have any children and he thought of you as his daughter." The lawyer continued, "he left fifty-five percent of the hospital to you, all his properties, which adds up to four and all the money he had in the bank. Moses left no debts."

Mary had a crying fit and Douglas didn't say a word. He let Mary get out all her sadness.

"I didn't want any of this. I just wanted them to be here with me. I loved them as if they were my parents." She said weeping and sobbing.

"They were aware of this, Mary. They loved you too. Sissy did not want to leave anything to her relatives who never came to visit them, and Moses only had a brother who was single and passed away before he made the will. I think it is nothing but fair to leave everything to you, Mary." Said the lawyer politely.

The lawyer left and Mary cried even more, feeling all the love and gratitude toward Moses and Sissy. They made her a rich woman.

Thank you, my parents and my dear friends. I will remember you for the rest of my life. One day we will be together again and have a great party. Rest in peace. Mary wiped her face that was wet with tears and decided to make some coffee. She needed to think about what to do.

She wouldn't want to be the hospital director, never! She liked to save lives, and as a director, she would have to give up all this and she wouldn't have time for anything else.

She was engaged and wanted to enjoy her life with Paul. To work and have a social life too. She saw how Moses was dedicated to the hospital and had no time for anything.

I'll find a good director to manage everything efficiently and professionally, thought Mary.

Paul called and Mary told him everything, sometimes crying and sometimes with great sadness.

Mary knew she'd have to be cold and decide everything quickly and efficiently. The hospital couldn't be without a director and she didn't want to leave it in the hands of someone incompetent.

She started going over all the doctors at the hospital and decided to give Robson a call.

"Good afternoon, Mary!" He said sadly.

"Hi Robson!" she said.

"So sad with all that happened, we're all very upset. Moses was a great friend and a wonderful director." He said with regret.

"Robson, can we meet today? If you don't have much on your plate at the hospital, I mean." She spoke sweetly.

"Sure! I've just left the office."

"Where are you? Do you want me to go to you?" he asked willingly.

"You'd do me a big favor if you could come to my apartment." She said with a sweet voice.

"Sure! I'll be there in 20 minutes."

Robson had been dating a nurse for six months and had

given up on Mary. *What's left is a great friendship*, he thought as he changed his clothes.

It took Robson half an hour to get to her apartment.

"Come in!" said Mary hugging and kissing her friend.

"I'm so sorry for your loss. We all know how cherished you were by Moses and Sissy." He said looking at Mary's sad face.

"Thank you, Robson! What I'm about to tell you must remain between us, for now." Mary said looking at him very seriously.

"Sure! What's happening?" he asked with a frowning worried expression.

"Would you like to be the new hospital director? Of course, I'll have to talk to the other shareholders first and see if they agree, but the last word will be mine."

"I don't understand," he said astonished.

"Well, I still have a meeting with the lawyer, but from what he told me, I'm Moses' only heir," Mary said as she started to weep.

Robson rose from his seat and hugged Mary's comforting her.

"Don't be like that darling, that's the way life is," he said in a faint voice.

"I'm so sad. I loved them like my parents."

"I know! I know! It's going to be all right," he said, patting her on the back.

"Let me think about it. As you know, it's a great responsibility and I'll have to give up being a doctor. I promise to give you an answer tomorrow. I thank you for trusting me."

Robson talked a little more with Mary, telling her about

his new girlfriend with enthusiasm.

Mary felt happy for her friend.

Chapter Twenty-One

SIX MONTHS LATER

Mary was happy and grateful. In since the passing of her friends, she found out she was very rich and that she would no longer have to work if she didn't want to.

Moses had left her quite well off. Robson took over the hospital administration with the endorsement of everyone else. After this period, everyone was satisfied and happy to have Robson. He turned into an excellent director and the hospital was doing better every day and making good earnings.

"Thirty days left till your wedding, dear, how do you feel?" asked her mother.

"I'm so happy, Mom," Mary answered with a smile, tasting her vanilla ice cream.

"Mary! You're going to get fat like that. What are you so anxious about, dear?" her mother was laughing.

"Mom, I miss Moses and Sissy so much, and I never thought they were going to make me so rich. I'm so grateful to them." Mary said looking at her mother.

"They loved you, darling, and they had no one to leave their fortune to. You were their best friend. Don't feel guilty about benefiting from that money."

"I'm not going to. I Promise!" said Mary calmly.

The days flew by and Mary was more and more wrapped up in the preparations for her wedding.

Paul was excited and he had never been happier.

They decided that they would go on living in Paul's penthouse and Mary would leave her apartment ready for when they had any relatives or friends over.

Debby was five months pregnant and had a huge belly, as there were two babies, much to Wagner's delight.

She and Wagner would be Mary and Paul's bride's maid and best man. The big day arrived.

"Calm down, Paul, continue like this and you'll have a breakdown," Wagner said, fixing his friend's tie.

"I don't understand. My whole life, I've been putting on and take off ties and now I can't tie that damn knot," he said with a smile from ear to ear.

"You're very nervous. It's going to be all right." Wagner said, smiling at his best friend.

Paul was elegantly dressed and very handsome. He resembled a Greek god!

He was at the altar waiting for Mary, who was five minutes late. The anxiety was enormous, but he knew it would be worth it.

The wedding march began to play and everyone looked back. Mary appeared at the big church door with her mother by her side. They'd go in hand in hand.

Mary was magnificent! She was wearing a champagne dress and her hair was loose around her face with a beautiful tiara.

Her makeup was very light and she glowing with happiness.

When Paul spotted Mary holding hands with her mother, he began to cry looking at his beloved, and Wagner offered him a handkerchief.

I love you so much, Mary, Paul thought wiping his eyes. Mary smiled at everyone and upon arriving at the altar her mother kissed her on the cheek and hugged her.

"I wish you all the happiness in the world, Mary," she said thrilled. Mary just smiled at her and went to meet her beloved.

The ceremony was beautiful, and the priest spoke of all the things that go into a lasting relationship.

Mary cried and so did Paul.

The reception was wonderful, and everyone had fun until late at night. Mary and Paul took Mary's private jet and they went to spend their honeymoon in Paris.

They spent a week visiting museums and eating the best French food. They both needed a break after going through so many things.

"I can't believe we've been here three days, honey," Mary said, sipping her ice cream.

"Time flies beside you, dear," said Paul giving Mary a kiss.

"Paul, I have a project in my mind and would like to

hear your opinion and, if you have time, I would like to count on your help as well.

"What do you have in mind?" he gave Mary his full attention.

"How about we both open a rehab clinic for the homeless." She said looking at him.

"Mary? That's all I ever wanted, but I always lacked money for it." Paul said thrilled.

"Moses left me with a lot of money, and even if I live to be a hundred, I would never be able to spend it all." She said very seriously. "I would very much like to help people who really want to get out of this life in the streets."

"We could ask for tax incentives, partner with the government and also with industries and factories that want to offer positions to people like that. How about that?" Paul was very excited.

"Sure. I agree we should partner, and I also want to talk to the shareholders of the hospital so we can assist this population for free. With full-time psychiatrists and psychologists. I will set aside an area to treat these people." Mary and Paul made a lot of plans and Paul loved and admired Mary more and more for her generosity.

"Paul? How about we sell that jet?" She asked smiling.

"It would be good money for our project. You can count on me, love, leave the red tape to me."

"I'm going to meet with everyone and give you an answer, we have a lot of friends who are rich and can help us. I want a hospital, where there will be treatment, leisure, education, and also a children's ward."

"How about we had a wing dedicated to women who were victims of domestic violence? They would stay long enough to settle down," Paul said excitedly.

"Together with their kids?" asked Mary.

"Of course!" Paul replied.

"Let's give it some thought, honey, and see the best way to do it. There is no way we could mix these women and their children with those addicted to drugs." Mary said thoughtfully.

"That's right, it would have to be well apart, anyway. It was just an idea, dear." He spoke.

"In fact, it was a great idea, but we need to take it easy. I appreciate your enthusiasm and dedication to this project."

Mary was excited and happy like never before and Paul thought he was the luckiest man in the world.

"Have you thought of a name yet?" Paul asked with a smile.

"Sure. We'll call it John's Institute." Mary looked at Paul with love.

Paul filled his eyes with tears and hugged Mary.

"Honey, I don't deserve you." He said moved by what she had just told him.

We're going to name this house after your brother, and wherever he is, I'm sure he is going to help us to always reach for the best.

"Thank you, Mary, for all your love, affection and friendship. I will always love you from the bottom of my heart."

"I love you, Paul." Mary looked at him and she knew that

they would be very happy.

They both enjoyed the best of Paris. They spent days strolling everywhere, they made love as much as they could and the day came returning them back to their responsibilities.

Mary arrived at the hospital and went straight to the operating room. The man shot in the abdomen had little chance to make it, but she never gave up on a patient and surely this one would survive.

It was a difficult and complicated surgery, but she knew she could make a difference in people's lives.

Mary called Jason to help her with the John Institute project and he said he would be honored to help.

"My dear, I'll be glad to join in; it'll be my pro bono project. I've always wanted to help improve our society." Jason said to Mary.

"Thank you, darling." Mary thanked him with a hug and a kiss on his cheek.

They'd become good friends and always went out to have some wine. Jason had a great girlfriend and Paul accompanied them whenever he could.

Mary and Paul were impressed with their friends' reaction. Everyone they invited to be part of John Institute's millionaire venture insisted on charging nothing for their participation. So far, they had only spent money on the purchase of a former orphanage decommissioned twenty-five years before.

The old house belonged to a family and the owner made a ridiculous offer after learning what it would be retrofitted for.

Help came from everywhere and Mary and Paul were delighted.

After the engineer said that it was better to bring everything down than to try to take advantage of some old walls, Mary and Paul decided to give the green light to the whole project and so it was done.

Jason also accompanied the works with all the dedication and care of a great and renowned architect.

Nothing that would be depressing or remind you of a hospital. It would all be decorated like a hotel.

Mary was delighted!

"This is going to be beautiful, my friends!" she said at every meeting.

"That's our goal," Jason said smiling, and the engineer couldn't agree more.

Before long, they could already inaugurate it and everything was going according to plan.

"Sit down here, dear," Mary spoke to Paul sweetly.

"You make me so happy!" Paul told Mary, kissing her lips with love and affection.

"You also make me happy, dear. Thank you for being you."

Mary and Paul sat facing the moon and nothing could make them any happier.

They both thanked God for that.

Chapter Twenty-Two

Preparations for the inauguration of John Institute were in full swing.

Paul worked every day after coming home from the office with the house/hospital implementation projects and the owner of the plot next to the orphanage, when he learned how important that project would be, he decided to donate it for Mary and Paul to do whatever they wanted.

They were beside themselves with joy, for there, apart from the whole John Institute, they would start Moses Institute that would be destined to women who suffered from domestic violence, with their children, for up to three months, to settle down, get a job and daycare or school for their children.

Wagner had partnered with them to employ in his companies people who had given up drugs, giving a second chance to those who longed for a better future.

Debby managed together with influential friends to partner with daycare centers and public schools for them to receive the children of women at risk. Everyone was striving to help Mary and Paul in their projects and when they realized Mary had used next to nothing of the money left by Moses, there were so many partnerships and donations that there was still a lot of money left, that really was a true miracle and Mary thanked God for it.

Both houses were in the finishing phase and the structures were magnificent. The city had never heard of such a wonderful project.

The state governor and the mayor decided to give them a hand and the tax incentives remained great.

Mary and Paul would pay neither electricity nor water from the houses; the government was making these two essential items available for free. Taxes wouldn't be charged either.

The governor managed to get MRI and CT machines as a donation from Germany. The mayor would donate these two super modern devices and the city hall wanted to score points with its voters. But, it was John Institute that ended up winning.

Jason would donate all the furniture to the Moses Institute, he insisted on that and Paul's and Mary's mothers would run this house.

The two were excited to be part of this project. They were both loving it.

"Dear?" Mary called Paul in a sweet voice.

"Yes, darling." Paul came out of his desk and went to Mary.

"Could you imagine that everything would work out

and that we would be so fortunate to receive so much support?" Mary asked Paul.

"Not in my sweetest dreams I thought we'd have so much support. Do you have any idea how many friends, real friends, we have that are involved in all this?" Paul went to his desk and took a spreadsheet to show Mary.

"I know there are many people involved, but I have no idea how many of them are our friends," Mary answered looking at him.

"Two hundred and five friends are collaborating somehow. By the way, we beat our friend Stanley in the donation of five hundred water fountains and disposable cups for ten years.

"Oh, my God, Paul, that's wonderful!" Mary said in awe, "When did Stanley decide to help us?"

He saw an announcement in the Times paper on our great work that we were doing, he was offended that we didn't look for him, can you believe it?" he is a good man and an extraordinary entrepreneur.

"Paul, we have left Moses' money practically untouched! That's wonderful because we can stay in business for years until we find more partners," Mary said very excitedly.

"Yes!" answered Paul.

"Paul?" called his friend Wagner terrified.

Paul's heart went off and he froze, already knowing that something bad had happened. "Talk to me," Paul said worriedly.

"Debby's in labor. We're going to the hospital."

"Take it easy, Mary and I are on our way," Paul said.

"What happened, dear," Mary asked, anxiously rising from behind her desk.

"Debby is on her way to the hospital; the twins are on their way." He said smiling happily. "Wagner is terrified," Paul smiled a fool as if the babies were his.

"Come on, baby! I'm going to help in the delivery."

They both left in a hurry and got there together with Wagner and Debby.

"Calm down, love, it's going to be all right," said Wagner as pale as a ghost, accompanied by the whole family.

"I'm fine honey, the contractions are not strong yet."

"Hey guys!" said Mary and Paul together.

"Oh! Thank God you're here," Wagner, said terrified as he was helping Debby get out of the car.

Debby looked at Mary and smiled to see Wagner so terrified and the whole family around them.

"Please make room for Debby. The orderly with the wheelchair is coming." Said Mary smiling at them.

"I want to see the birth and be by Debby's side," Wagner said looking at Mary, kind of asking for her permission.

"I think you'd better not go in, Wagner," said Paul, who knew his friend very well.

"No way, I'm going in. I will not leave Debby alone," said a terrified and distressed Wagner.

"I won't be alone, dear; Mary will be in there with me and my doctor, too," Debby spoke calmly.

"There's no way I'm leaving you."

"OK. Now that the wheelchair has arrived for Debby, this young man will escort you all to a room. She will stay there until the contractions become more regular and less than 5 minutes apart. Then we will go to the operating room." Mary explained, looking at the five members of Wagner's family.

Debby was in pain, but she didn't say anything. She was afraid Wagner would have a heart attack.

"Why did they all come? The whole family?" asked Mary amused in a low voice.

"No idea, honey," Paul said smiling too.

The hospital room soon became crowded with the five of them and Paul. Wagner wouldn't stay away from Debby and Paul smiled at his friend.

Mary was already in the operating room to make sure everything was ready.

"I can give her an epidural if you want, Alex," she told Debby's doctor.

"Please, do this, dear. I'm with another patient there, in the other room. She's not doing too well." He said quietly.

"Ok, you can count on it." Mary said calmly. Mary went back to the room and it was in real chaos with Wagner on top of Debby giving her no room to breathe, the kids talking loudly, and Paul just sitting and watching that hilarious scene.

"Everybody! Listen, please, you can all go down and I'll stay with Debby," she said gently.

They all looked at Wagner, whose eyes were wide open.

"I'm staying with Debby, Mary." Wagner said firmly and nothing would change his mind.

"I'll go down with the kids and wait downstairs," Paul said.

"No!" Wagner shouted, "you stay here with me, man," he said terrified.

"Darling, it's all right. There is no need to worry. It's going to be all right." Debby said taking his hand.

"Paul and I are staying, and the kids are going down. Mark, take care of your sisters."

"Sure, Daddy, I've got this," said Mark, already calling Cinthia and Anne down.

They all said goodbye to Debby with a kiss and hugs. Debby was tired and wanted privacy.

Mary looked at Paul for help to get Wagner away from there.

Paul smiled amusedly and shook his head, meaning there was nothing he could do. Mary gave up and walked away with Paul to stay by the window.

After thirty minutes, Debby was already well dilated and with many contractions.

Mary called the nurse with the anesthesia and told Debby to sit up, in the space between one contraction and another, she would give her the epidural anesthesia.

Debby sat down and Wagner positioned himself next to her.

When Mary went around the bed and took the syringe with a large needle and kept touching her fingers on Debby's back trying to find the best place to apply it, she looked scared at Wagner as he grew paler and paler.

"Hurry up, Paul!" she called. "Wagner is about to faint."

Before Wagner fell on the floor, Paul held him by his waist and laid him on the couch.

"Wagner!" called Paul terrified.

"That's why I don't like husbands in the operating room. You never know if you should help the husband or the patient," said Mary smiling.

"Is he going to be okay?" asked Debby in increasing pain.

"He's going to be fine, honey," Mary said delicately.

"I want to go to the bathroom, Mary," Debby said.

"Let's do the intestinal lavage now, before the anesthesia."

"Paul, please, leave for a moment, let Wagner sleep there. We need some privacy."

"I'll be out here. Anything you need, just call me." Paul replied politely, not looking at Debby who had his breasts on display and was sweating more than anything.

"Thank you, dear," Mary said already telling the nurse to start the lavage procedure in Debby.

Mary checked Wagner's pulse, and everything was fine. She'd let him get some sleep.

After all the procedures, Debby was ready, and the stretcher had arrived.

"Stay with Wagner, dear." said Mary taking Paul's hand and squeezing affectionately.

"Is he going to be okay?" asked Paul worried.

"Oh, yes, darling. Let him sleep a little. He was too terrified."

Paul looked at Wagner sleeping on the couch and sat on

a chair. He took his cell phone and started taking pictures of his friend and laughing.

Mary helped Debby's doctor and the twins were born beautiful and healthy.

Two beautiful boys. Mary helped clean them up and handed them to an emotional and crying Debby.

The twins cried loud and strong. Mary smiled as well.

"Congratulations, dear! You did great and your little children are beautiful."

"Thank you, Mary, for staying here with me. What about Wagner?" she asked smiling.

"Sleeping still." they both laughed.

"I'm going to give you some medication so you can sleep until Dr. Alex is done, okay?" said Mary giving her children to the nurse to weigh, bathe, and wrap them up in a warm blanket.

Debby nodded, she was exhausted, and she really wanted to get some sleep.

Epilogue

Wagner finally woke up.

"Where's Debby, Paul?" asked Wagner scared sitting on the couch, still feeling dizzy.

"You're the father of twins, Wagner," Paul told him smiling from ear to ear.

"Dad, did you also pass out when the three of us were born?" asked Anne laughing, and the three also laughed hugging a Wagner with his unkept hair.

"I'm feeling so ashamed," he said, standing up and recomposing himself in the best possible way.

He went to the bathroom and washed his face, ran his hands in his hair to try to look better.

"When can we see her?" Wagner asked Paul.

"I don't think now is a good time. Mary came by and said the boys are fine and so is Debby. First, she must move her legs and then she can come to the room." Paul said trying to calm him down.

"Can't we even see the twins?" he asked frustrated.

"In a while, Wagner, please sit-down," Paul said, smiling and the children hugged him smiling.

Wagner hugged his children and got much calmer.

"Let's go downstairs, have a cup of coffee, and then we'll come back," Paul said getting everyone out of the room.

Finally, everyone was able to go to Debby's room. The twins were breast-feeding in Debby, each on one side and she was in love with those cute little ones.

"Oh, my dear!" Wagner said, approaching her and giving her a tender kiss. He looked at his beautiful children and smiled, and at the same time, he cried like a baby.

"Daddy, it's all right!" Cynthia hugged him, and the others came and hugged the father, who was even more moved.

"It's all right, honey. Look how beautiful and strong they are." Debby told him without being able to hold Wagner's hand since she had her children in her arms.

"Mary's already getting you a senior nursing student to help you at home, okay, honey?"

"Thank you, dear. I'm really going to need it," she said with a smile. The babies were beautiful, strong, and healthy and Debby and Wagner couldn't be happier.

Four months went by flying and Wagner and Debby were happy and increasingly in love.

The house was full of toys and children's stuff everywhere. But Wagner didn't care, he was happy to be a father again and everyone at home was eager to help Debby with whatever it took.

She decided to hire two nannies and let go of the student who had almost no experience.

Debby intended to stay with her children for another three months and then go back to work. She'd work at her home office then go back to the office.

Wagner never suggested Debby should quit her job to take care of their children.

That would certainly never happen. Debby loved being a lawyer and wouldn't give it up for all the money in the world, but, of course, now that she was a mother, she would have to give more assistance to her children and organize her schedule in a way that she could do both activities well.

Time went by and after six months of the twins' birth, the big day finally came.

John Institute and Moses Institute would both be inaugurated on December 24.

Mary, Paul, and their numerous friends who contributed to the project were all looking forward to the inauguration.

It was a beautiful reception with many important people like the governor, the mayor, and many other influential and politicians of the city.

Mary and Paul knew the importance of these people in making both institutions work with as little money as possible.

Mary made a point of keeping it in as a community-run property; this was not debatable.

The two houses were beyond expectations in terms of structure, equipment, and health professionals.

"Attention, please! May I have your attention, please!" said Mary into the microphone next to Paul. The buzz ceased and she started.

I would like to thank each of you here and say that this dream is not only mine and Paul's, but it is of all of us.

"Hurray!" people screamed. Mary smiled.

"If today this dream is being fulfilled, it is thanks to each one of us that we strive in some way. Whether you're donating money, getting a sponsor, or donating your time."

"Hurray!" There was a standing ovation.

"I want to ask everyone to come and visit us, come and be part of John Institution and the Moses Institution. Come and be a volunteer, with a friendly word, with donations of clothing and footwear, which surely our less fortunate brothers will need when they arrive here. The fight will be long and hard, but I know that with God's help and with your help, we will succeed.

The fight is just beginning. I thank you all from the deepest of my heart. May God grant each one of you the reward you are worthy of."

Mary cried and everyone who was present felt grateful that she had done something to try to help.

"Happy?" asked Paul hugging Mary.

"Yes, I am very happy and grateful to you all."

Mary and Paul hugged and were certain of a happy ending for everyone.

The End

About the Author

Ana C. Sales was born and lives in Goiânia, Goiás with her husband.

Ana has four children, and is the owner of the renowned pastry studio, La Gourmet Doces.

Ana is also the author of:

A Ponte que Eu Não Atravessei

The Greystones - Se Apaixone por eles.
The Greystones - Fall in Love with Them.

Um Amor para Doutora Mary Taylor

About 5310 Publishing: Canadian-based, 5310 Publishing has operations worldwide, selling books in 127 countries and multiple languages. Since 2018, 5310 has published adult, young adult, and colouring books.

Follow us on Twitter and Instagram: @5310publishing
For more books, go to 5310publishing.com

If you enjoyed this book, please review it.